STAND
UP

Also by Nikesh Shukla

Run, Riot
The Boxer

STAND UP

NIKESH SHUKLA

Hodder
Children's
Books

HODDER CHILDREN'S BOOKS

First published in Great Britain in 2023 by Hodder & Stoughton

1 3 5 7 9 10 8 6 4 2

A CIP catalogue record for this book is available from the British Library.

ISBN 978 1 444 96989 4

Typeset in Din by Avon DataSet Ltd, Alcester, Warwickshire

Printed and bound in Great Britain by Clays Ltd, Elcograf S.p.A.

The paper and board used in this book
are made from wood from responsible sources.

Hodder Children's Books
An imprint of Hachette Children's Group
Part of Hodder & Stoughton Limited
Carmelite House
50 Victoria Embankment
London EC4Y 0DZ

An Hachette UK Company
www.hachette.co.uk
www.hachettechildrens.co.uk

For Bisha and Saima, for always standing up
and for always being generous and hilarious.

1

I'll tell you a secret, ladies and gentlemen.

I think dogs are fine.

I don't hate them. I don't love them. I don't run at the sight of a dog. I don't get into in-depth conversations about cutesy habits and ages and breeds with dog owners as I pet their dog and make the assumption it's consensual.

I do none of these things.

Because . . .

I think dogs are fine. They're OK. They're just there.

I can't believe this, of all things, is probably my most controversial opinion. I know dog owners definitely think the world loves dogs as much as they do, those slobbering, stingy, needy little beasts . . . am I right . . .? I know dog owners would be like, I understand you hate my dog, I understand you're scared of the concept of dogs, but to be fifty-fifty? That's outrageous. You are a monster, ma'am. I get how sociopathic I sound . . . to dog owners. But I will not be judged by anyone who lets their dog kiss them with tongues on the mouth.

Yes. Yes, I am. I am a dog-agnostic monster lady.

Dognostic. That's me.

I look at the word 'dognostic' and think about how to build up to the second saying of it, so it has maximum impact. I add an exclamation mark so I know to really hit it. It still needs a killer punchline.

'Madhu,' I hear whispered to me and I look up as Shanai hovers by my desk. She picks up the UCAS book I was idly flicking through before having this flash of stand-up genius and reads intently till I clear my throat and close the notebook.

'Hey, Shanai, you OK?'

She shakes her head. Of course she's not. She's here for advice, probably, because she's arguing with her boyfriend. For some reason, she thinks I am good with advice. Usually it's because I listen and she talks her own way to a solution eventually. And I then affirm her solution and she thanks me like I'm a genius.

I love her but I really want to nail this stand-up set before tonight.

'Marvin is being so distant at the moment,' Shanai says. 'He replies to all my texts with one- or two-word answers and when I ask what's wrong, he always says, "Nothing, babe, all is calm" and I'm like, "Marvin we're not connecting" . . .' She pauses. 'I should just give him space, yeah? Let him come to me when he's ready.'

'That's what I would do,' I say, smiling widely. I want to giggle because I probably would have told her to tell him to not be such an idiot and threaten to stop going out with him.

'I think he's cheating on me with this girl, Pri. She works with him at the trainer shop.'

I shake my head. 'Marvin is a lot of things,' I say. 'But he's not a cheater. I swear to you, he's fine. I honestly think he's too chaotic to cheat. Being a good cheater requires a lot of admin. I don't know if he'd be able to handle any of that. Just talk to him.'

Shanai says thanks and puts the university directory down on the table and leaves the library. I pat the archaic booklet and smile. I know it's all online but sometimes, when you want to look busy, so no one knows you're writing jokes, you need the thick books in front of you.

I look at the clock. One more hour to go before I can bounce by Pizza City to get my paycheque and express irritation at Danny for paying us with this parchment that indicates how much money we have earned this past fortnight. I may like physical books, but electronic banking is just, well, instant.

After I get paid, I'm going to go and do my stand-up. I cannot wait. Also, I am terrified.

Bristol is extra tonight. All the students are back in town after the Christmas break. They swarm the centre. I'm doing Super Mario-level dodging to make it through alive. The extra-ness of trying to muddle through the crowd is making me sweat through layers of clothes. I can feel a straight line down my spine that is melded to my T-shirt. It feels gross and slimy against the warmth of my padded coat. I'm glad I didn't wear white. I'm glad I went for a plain black tee. Strong look for my mission tonight. Serious. Timeless. That's the energy of the black tee.

Beyond the students is a circle of skateboarders, all sitting on the floor spotlit by the tall streetlights, panting, sharing round a water bottle, laughing and reminding each other of the cool swizzles and spinnies and falls they all just did. (Swizzles and spinnies. Don't let my knowledge of skateboarding intimidate you, folks). One guy is icing his knee. Another has blood all down his white tee. He's smiling and you can see how busted-up his lip is.

Then it's the Bristol lads who wear their long wool coats open, revealing casual shirts (vertical stripes), tucked into stonewashed jeans that flare out ever so slightly on to pointy brown shoes. They're all red-faced from the drinky-drinks and I'm like, it's not even 8 p.m., bruv.

Winter makes people go feral. It's like, all that family stress at Christmas leads you into a January where you're both skint and desperate to cut loose. I pop into the pizza restaurant and Danny greets me by the door with an envelope. Danny is only a year older than me. He left school to run the family business, now manages the family business, and does it well by employing a steady stream of hilarious young people like me to give the type of service that Yelp describes as 'spiky and entertaining'. Also by making the best pizzas in the centre of Bristol. He hasn't changed the menu since his dad retired back to the old country. When Danny said that, I assumed Italy, cos, you know, pizza and generalisations. But Danny's half-Indian, so I then assumed there. Turns out the old country is . . . Devon, cos that's where old people retire. Danny's dad, a legend of the Bristol restaurant scene, comes in every other Thursday to do the books.

'Thanks, Danny,' I say as he passes me my envelope. I make the same joke I do every time. 'I can't wait to get paid like it's 1981. See you . . .'

'Well, actually,' Danny says, slinking one hand over his long, gelled hair, pulled back into a teeny tiny bun at the nape of his beautiful hairless neck. 'You have a shift tonight.'

I shake my head. 'No can do, Danny Boy. I swapped with Carina. I'm doing . . . a thing tonight.'

Danny straightens himself. He's small so this is his way of asserting authority, to appear slightly taller than he is but still shorter than the rest of us.

'It's Friday night,' he says. 'You always work Friday nights.'

'And Carina is covering my shift.'

He clears his throat.

'What are you doing tonight? Hot date? Or finally doing your uni application? Which ones did you settle on?'

Danny splashes olive oil in his hands from a nearby plastic squeezy bottle and clasps them together. He returns to kneading dough, murmuring along to some Migos song playing on the kitchen speakers. Meanwhile, I'm hyperventilating at the mention of my uni application as it really is the iceberg to my luxury cruise liner.

I lie and say I have a family thing.

2

The comedy club is in the cafe of The Station, the youth club none of my college peers would ever venture to, cos they all go to the one near college with more space and free music studios. I'm glad because I want to start incognito, find my feet before the people who know me see. The night is called LOLZ, because the youth worker who set it up was probably trying to be relatable. It's cute. My stomach feels like it has a fizzing Berocca tablet in it, bouncing up and down and around.

I cannot believe I'm about to debut my stand-up comedy and I am terrified. I've been waiting for this moment for so long. My entire life even. Definitely the last six years. Which is, like, a third of my life so far.

Let's say it again. For emphasis. Tonight, I am doing my first stand-up set ever.

I know you're sitting here thinking, hold up, this person is hilarious. No way it's her *first time*. She's a seasoned professional . . . right?

OK, so here's what you need to know about me: I'm seventeen and a comedy god . . . in waiting. TBC and all that. But I know

I'm pretty funny. I have two and a half terms left before going uni. To most likely do law, of all things. I mean, I love an argument, I am titillated by debate, but a life in the law? Not my choice. It was Papa's dream. He runs a corner shop and every evening tells us how tired he is and how much he regrets not becoming a lawyer, before reminding me he never had the opportunity.

Papa pinned all his hopes on my older sis, Meena, but then she failed him. And now it's all down to me.

Before she left for London, Meena said, 'Look, if I don't conform, that sets the precedent for you to do whatever you want, innit.'

I wish I'd know then that this myth of the older sibling as rebel is a lot of rubbish, man. Seriously. Literally, Papa just decided, nope nope nope, double down on the strictness and expectation and oh hey, no pocket money for you; you earn it but never take your eyes off my prize.

Sorry for all the info-dumping, ladies and gentlemen. It's not bad exposition, it's just, I need to catch you up a little and rather than showing you how crazy life was before I decided to laugh it all away with stand-up, it's just easier to tell you, you know? Is that bad comedy? Is referencing it even worse? Who cares? You're laughing!

I have one of those origin stories that most actual proper comedians will relate to. I'm a dark-skinned Asian and that makes me the target of all sorts of racist jokes, terrible colourism and bad comedy. Especially in school where my class was filled with light-skinned brownies and white people.

This girl at school, Hannah, used to call me Miss Negative cos she said I looked like one of those old camera films. I can remember the chants: 'Miss Negative, Miss Negative, click click click, it's Miss Negative.'

I remember one day coming in to find everyone in class, even the brown boys, all with boot polish on their faces. *Even the brown boys.* I was so angry, I just lost it and started letting loose, telling them all exactly what I thought. The thing was, they all started laughing as I rinsed each of them. I discovered I could make people laugh. And if I was making them laugh, they weren't making me cry. So pathetic, eh? My love of comedy, my love of joy-spreading comes from being bullied in school. It sucks, but ask any comedian and I guarantee the real oddballs are the ones who used humour to stop themselves being rinsed, beaten up, bullied or mocked. Cos if I was mocking them, I was de-arming them and charming them all at once. It's so grim that it works like that.

They eventually stopped calling me Miss Negative because they were scared of what I might say back in return. Didn't solve the racism and colourism, but it did save me a little, I guess.

About six years ago, a Spotify playlist I was listening to, made by a musician I liked at the time, went from a track by Best Coast to a track by Kareena Patel. From her stand-up album. It was jarring to go from Bethany Cosentino singing about wishing she had a boyfriend to hearing someone talk really fast about dumping a boyfriend because he compared the

8

toilet seat being up or down to a glass being half full or half empty. She dumped him cos he was stupid.

I can remember that first line so well: *God, I can't even tell you how dumb this guy I was up until quite recently seeing is . . . Actually, I can and I will. Strap in . . .*

And I laughed. Oh, how I laughed. I'd never even had a boyfriend before at that point. But I laughed.

And laughed. And laughed. And then I listened to it again. And I laughed, and laughed and laughed and I clicked on her name, Kareena Patel, and discovered a whole album of her talking to make people laugh.

Can you actually believe this was a job, ladies and gentlemen? My mind was blown. It still is. Someone paid her money to talk at people and make them laugh.

I got obsessed. I listened to everything of hers I could find, and then I found camera-phone YouTube videos. And she was just so effortlessly good. So funny. Everything she said was about her, her life, her parents, her inability to fit in, how she thought everyone around her was dumb, how she was the only one who could put the world back together. The way she left the microphone on the stand but used pauses to pace the stage. The way she always wore a black T-shirt and white Converse. The way she stood. The way she winked at the camera. The way she had the same immigrant-parent references as me.

I discovered more comedians just like her. All these amazing people who told jokes. Made people laugh. And most of all told the truth about themselves. That was the sad thing about me rinsing all those people who called me Miss Negative. I never even got to tell them how messed up it was what they did. Instead, I had to insult their looks, their aptitude, their rich dads buying their way through life. I then started filling out books with jokes, sets, riffs, stuff that I never said out loud. I have seven books filled with comedy that hasn't yet seen the light of day.

When I decided I was going to do this LOLZ set at The Station – just to get the jokes out there – I grabbed my notebooks off my shelf and cobbled together the perfect set, almost so I could say goodbye to all these pages before heading uni.

I remember the first joke I ever made up. Before I even knew it was a career. Before I knew you could be paid to tell jokes. I told my dad one day over breakfast, as he made his world-famous scrambled eggs with haldi and chilli and spring onions and coriander, 'Papa, what happened to the sheep that fell in the sea?'

He stopped and looked at me, hunched over the hob, about to pour chai into a cup.

'I don't know, bwana,' he said. He loves throwing Swahili words into conversation to remind everyone he is Kenyan Indian. Even though bwana means mister, he still calls all of us that. It's his way of showing affection. 'What happened to the sheep that fell in the sea?'

'It grew baaaaaaaa-nacles.'

I burst out laughing. I couldn't stop. I was ten. I was creasing so much, shuddering till my laugh was silent and it was all in the shake of my shoulders. I held my hips, almost to stop my sides from splitting.

Papa stopped stirring and turned to me.

'I don't understand . . .'

'Baaaa-nacles . . . Papa, do I need to . . . ?'

'Bwana, how does a sheep fall in the sea? They're not stupid. Why are they at the beach?'

I rolled my eyes. *Papa, it's not that deep. Why are you tearing apart my joke?*

'OK, OK, Papa, fine. What happened to the sheep at the bottom of the sea?'

'What?'

'It grew baaaaaaaa-nacles.'

I burst out laughing again. I was out of control. Papa smiled this time.

I continued, through my tears. 'What happened to the cow at the bottom of the sea?'

Papa shrugged, shaking his head like I was nuts.

'It grew moooo-ssels.'

Papa smiled, but he wasn't really smiling.

'And . . .' I couldn't breathe. This was the funniest moment of my entire life so far. 'What happened to the goat at the bottom of the sea?'

'I don't know, Madhu,' he said, using my name to show me enough was very nearly enough, quite frankly.

'It died,' I said, with the straightest face I could muster.

And he corpsed. My dad doubled over, laughing, dropping the sloppy wooden spoon of scrambled drippings on to the floor. He banged the worktop. Mum started screaming from her bedroom, cos she just loooooves shouting across the house, demanding to know what was going on.

And I laughed with him.

It was like he saw me for who I was.

God, I loved making him laugh that day. With a rule-of-three joke I didn't even realise was *one of the rules of comedy* and everything. Years later, I read about what I had done. You set up the joke, you then confirm the joke and then you change the joke. So, man walks down the street, slips on a banana skin. He walks down another street, tries to avoid the banana skin and slips on it, and then the third time, man walks down the street, steps carefully over the banana skin but falls down a manhole. A rule of three, comedy nerds.

Then, two years later, I discovered Kareena Patel, and I knew. Stand-up was my life. I needed to listen to and watch everything. Thank god for the Netflix stand-up specials. Except the ones by white dudes who want to say offensive things and call the show 'Triggered' or something, like they wanna be an edgelord whose only function is to tell jokes designed to wind people up and then shout at them if they don't find it funny.

As I enter the cafe, I realise that it's busier than usual. There's actually people in here for once. I purposefully chose this open-mic night for a reason. And that reason is, no audience.

It's a lot of pressure otherwise. A lot of pressure. I was expecting there to be, like, ten people here, basically five open-mic people, whatever mates they could muster and the compère.

I come to this event religiously and every time I think, *This is it, tonight I'm going to jump up and do my jokes*.

Except, I never do. I bottle it *every week*.

This time is different. I'm definitely doing it. I promise. Seriously. What's changed, you ask? The UCAS deadline is approaching faster than a flicked bogey, and something within me went, *It's now or never, sis*.

But as soon as I see the stage, I start to panic. There's too many people. They'll all be looking at me. The skin on my arms starts to itch.

'Hey Madhu,' I hear and turn to see who's calling me.

Leila, the barista, comes over. She used to be in college with me, the year above. We never spoke until one day I made her laugh. She was once standing amongst a group of people I was talking at by doing impressions of a posh actor saying racist stuff on television. And she was laughing with everyone else, and I was very aware that she was the only brown girl present, and I desperately wanted the solidarity of her friendship. She nodded and I nodded as the circle dissipated.

We nodded at each other every time we passed each other, after that. Right up until her last day of college.

And then she was gone. And the brown-girl solidarity in the corridors was over until Shanai changed colleges to mine, cos – well, let's just say, the school she was at did not want to change its name from Colston Academy, and that is messed-up, dude.

Leila and I didn't talk until I started rocking up to LOLZ to watch the comedians.

It wasn't even a barrier, that we hadn't talked at school. That first time I went in, I saw her and she said, 'Madhu, right? St Brendan's Sixth Form,' and I was like, 'Hey Leila,' and that was enough.

Brown-girl solidarity back in action. School just wasn't the place for us. It needed us both to leave before we could be pals. Since that first time I came in, she's been my bar buddy, watching over me as I studied the open-mic losers, making notes or writing sketches of jokes on my phone, chatting to me in breaks about her new girlfriend, about co-habitation problems, like cleaning the shower and other things I don't have to worry about because my mother cannot delegate, so I don't have to do anything at home.

She tried to convince me I should go up after I read her one of my jokes.

'No thanks.' I had said. Quickly.

'You deserve to experience someone who looks like you telling the jokes you want to hear, instead of these indistinguishable white boys . . .'

She was right.

I'm going to tell you a bitter truth that too often goes unsaid in this world.

Men. Aren't. Funny.

I have never met a man funnier than me. Than my friends. Than my mum. And she's my mum. No one finds their mum funny.

'You are definitely going up tonight,' Leila says this time.

The definitiveness of it makes me panic a bit. And even though I arrived with every intention of going up, it's like the bug eyes of Leila, through the expanse of her big glasses, make me crumble a bit. Like an ant through a magnifying glass on a hot summer's day in a cartoon.

Can I do this? Should I?

'OK,' I say. Then, uncontrolled, I add, 'Wait, I'm not sure . . .'

I'm already talking myself out of it. *Not this week*, my brain instructs.

'You have to,' Leila tells me. 'This is the week . . .'

'You're not my real dad,' I reply and look over my shoulder at the exit. At full acceleration, I could be there in under five seconds. I live my life a quarter mile at a time, Dominic Torretto-style. I'm not going up. Tonight's not the night. It feels off. I need it to be my decision. Not anyone else's.

'Listen, Madhu . . .'

'Listen, Leila, I'm not feeling it . . .'

Leila places a finger to my lips and I want to tell her to moisturise but she shushes me.

'Sam just realised it's all white dudes and Jazz who signed up for the open mic . . .'

'So, all white dudes . . .'

'Exactly,' Leila says, laughing.

Jazz is a brown guy comedian who does not want anyone to realise he's brown. The accent, the khakis, the shrill Asian auntie impression he does. It's all for the whites. I tell ya. 'I'm not being the token wimmins up there. They need to address that . . .'

The more it rolls around in my head, the more I think tonight is not the night. If I'm the only girl up there, it just adds a weird pressure for me. The first time needs to feel unpressured. Maybe I can sneak back into the restaurant before my replacement arrives and just work my shift. I don't want to do Sunday anyway. Sunday afternoons in a pizza restaurant are the pits. Divorced dads slumped over their phones while their obnoxious kids throw all their food on the floor.

Leila thinks for a second. 'You have to go up.'

'It's my first ever five minutes. I can't. Seriously. They'll be merciless. Also, I'm not being anyone's token. I'm not ready . . .'

'Let me tell you a secret,' she says, serious face on. 'No one is ever really ready. You know that bit in *When Harry Met Sally* when he goes, "when you realise you want to spend the rest of your life with someone, you want it to start right now"?'

'No,' I say. 'That film is old enough to be my real dad.'

'Madhu, come on. You have to . . .'

'They'll murder me.'

Leila shakes her head.

I turn to the door. Leila grabs my hand.

'Sam, this is Madhu, a hilarious new comic. She's going up tonight . . .'

'I—' I start to say to Leila, but Sam talks over me.

'Oh, hey, yes, the girl comic. Thank you so much. That'd be awesome, thank you,' he says in his most sincere voice, probably because he knows I'm ultimately saving him from looking bad.

He hands me a clipboard and asks me to sign my name.

This is madness. I swear.

I push the clipboard back to him. Leila takes the clipboard and starts filling it out herself. I try to pull it from her but she retreats to behind the counter. Sam, awkward and unsure whether the conversation is done, smiles and starts doing an exaggerated, bad moonwalk backwards.

I'm standing there by myself, thinking, *What are you even doing?*

Papa would kill me if he knew I was here.

Law degree, my brain reminds me.

I start edging towards the door, in full panic. My mind is racing. I didn't want this to be a thing. I just wanted to scratch an itch. Get it out of my system. So I can go uni knowing I did it.

I remember listening to Kareena Patel talking about what she referred to as 'the curiosity gap'.

'Like, every time a waiter puts a plate in front of you and tells you to be careful because it's hot, that's like life in so many ways,' she once said. 'Because we can only really understand how hot, and what he means by hot and what we mean by hot through experience. And isn't that the ultimate expression of life? What does not trying really mean? It means, I am willing to take the waiter's word for it that the plate is hot. Do you want to live your life this way? I don't. And three skin grafts later, you can barely tell, right?'

I see Jazz standing by the toilets. He's got his earbuds in and he's mouthing some words over and over. I've seen him three times and he's done the exact same set each time. He's probably gonna do it tonight. Why waste anyone's time with fresh jokes? He's doing hand signals to hammer home a punchline. I realise he's listening to a recording of his own material.

Oh no, I think. *I need to remind myself of what I'm going to say.*

I run to a dark corner of The Station and sit down, flicking through my notebook, squinting in the light of my phone torch.

Sam clears his throat.

'Jeez,' I shout loudly, dropping my phone and notebook into the darkness of this unnecessarily dim cafe. My heart is pounding.

'I don't know how that happened,' he says. 'It's so weird. Usually we have a girl . . .'

'Maybe there's, like, a big coven AGM or something?' I reply.

'Yeah, maybe. Look, if you're here, you'd be helping out big time . . .'

'Helping out?' I say.

'It's just . . . it doesn't look good . . .'

'So, you want me to help you look good?'

'Yes. Well actually, diversity is *so* important.'

'Right . . .' I say. 'I'm not feeling it.'

Sam leans forward and closes his eyes like I'm really stressing him out.

'You don't have to go on,' he says.

'I know,' I reply. 'And that would suck for you more than it would for me. I've never been up.'

'O-kay,' he says, hesitantly. Before getting increasingly aggressive. 'You're right. We need you. Last time this happened, we got murdered by some sixth form college paper in their lead column.' I cringe, because it was my college, and I know who wrote the piece. 'And yeah, I know, Leila said it'll be your first time . . .' Sam carried on, 'But look, it's just like any other gig. You were going to go up anyway. What's the difference?'

I hate that I'm giving him what he wants. I hate it. I hate that he's pushing me into this.

I see my phone light up and I pick it off the floor, dusting it off. It's a message from Papa. He's sent me a link to a profile of a Conservative MP who started his career as a barrister. Also brown.

This is my life. This is what's expected.

I delete the text. I never want to read about this evil Tory, ever.

'Fine,' I say eventually, leaving the longest pause I can. 'I'll be your token girl . . .'

'And you're brown as well,' Sam says, smiling, thinking he's in on a joke. 'Tick. And tick.'

19

'Are you serious, bro?' I say. I look out to an imaginary camera, like I'm in *The Office*.

Sam holds his hands up to say he's sorry, which is a power move because it means he doesn't need to actually say the words 'I'm sorry'.

'Tick those diversity boxes,' I say. Sam's pen is hovering. He just needs me to say yes and tell him my name. 'Tick. And tick. My name's Madhu.'

I spell it for him. Twice. I add a circumflex on the 'a' the second time, just to be fancy.

He stands up and Leila comes over, offering me a high five. I look at her elbow, because that's the way to ensure you never miss, and we give fives like pros.

'Wear this,' Leila says when Sam leaves, and shoves a black item of clothing at me. I open it up. It's a sweatshirt that says, in huge white letters, TOKEN.

'Oh wow,' I say, laughing. 'This is *a lot*.'

'It belongs to my friend Jacob – he's an artist who made it for such occasions as this. He left it here last night. I don't think he'd mind.'

I look up at the stage and that familiar ouchy churn hits my stomach. Suddenly my bag, filled with the UCAS directory and the anvil of an unwritten personal statement feels too much to carry. I pull my bag off and as I place it on the sticky floor by my feet, I hear someone say, 'Hey.'

I turn and see Jazz.

In his khaki trousers, sensible light-blue shirt and blue

blazer. He looks like a young trust-fund bro rather than a young Jerry Seinfeld, which is probably the look he's going for. Instead, he just looks like he's wearing his dad's clothes to his uncle's last-minute wedding.

'Jazz, right? Hi,' I say, extending a hand. 'My uncle has that exact same blazer.'

Jazz laughs. 'I hear you're finally going up,' he says. 'Sick uncle burn. Who did you come dressed as? A cool indie band member?'

'Is that . . . an insult?' I say, and Jazz laughs, realising his return burn failed. He steps back and puts his hands in his pockets like he's about to offer me unwanted advice.

I nod. I nod again. And then to really ram the point home I say, 'Yup,' slowly.

'It's good you're a woman because that'll really distract from the whole two Asians thing,' he says. Then he laughs. 'One Asian is tokenism. Two is diversity . . .'

'Three is white genocide,' I say, and he laughs. 'WHITE GENOCIDE,' I scream, like I'm in a heavy metal band, offering Jazz the horns of the devil on my index and teeny tiny finger, and his hands are out of his pockets and on his chest as he laughs.

His face really opens up when he laughs. For a comedian, he never does, though. He's so stiff and serious.

He has the floppy hair of the American comic, the white sneakers and khakis of the American comic. The delivery of the American comic. But the laugh of an Asian kid from the ends. A nasal 'hihihihihihi'.

'You should laugh more,' I say. 'You seem less like someone who dresses like my uncle.'

I laugh to show him I'm joking. I love you, Mukesh kaka! I'm just being silly!

'As I said,' he says. 'Just really lean into the woman thing. Don't steal any of my Asian thunder.'

'Oh, to be complex and nuanced and both an Asian and a woman and just *be* . . . What a dream to have . . .' I say and Jazz snaps his fingers, one, two, three, like we're at a jazz poetry evening.

'Good luck tonight,' Jazz says, sweetly.

'OK, Jazz, listen, go and stand over there. I'm not trying to be rude but I've literally never done stand-up before and I need to concentrate before I go humiliate myself.'

'That's the spirit,' Jazz says, pumping a fist into a thumbs up. I laugh as he backs away like a malfunctioning robot.

Leila joins me and hands me a fizzy water.

'God, he's fit,' she murmurs.

'He dresses like my uncle,' I reply.

'I bet your uncle's fit too,' Leila says, sighing deeply.

'Good evening and welcome to LOLZ, live from The Station . . .' Sam says, before making a couple of jokes about being down with the kids to a smattering of groans and titters. The energy is low so he breaks into his rap about how to make the perfect sandwich. Why are white men so desperate to do knowingly bad raps to show they sort of know all the

22

words to the *Fresh Prince* theme tune?

I'm getting more and more jittery because it's fuller than usual. There are at least twenty audience members who are just here to attend. They are all facing the stage and they are quiet. I look over at Leila for comfort as she serves teas, coffees and cakes. She loves stand-up nights. No one orders drinks cos they don't want the steam from the coffee machine to distract a comic who might then jump on the opportunity to make fun of them. She has literally nothing to do except learn Spanish on her phone app. Sometimes, if the silence falls just right, you can hear her whispering, 'Yo como manzanas,' into her phone.

I see her staring at the screen, mouthing some words.

I think about how to reply to Papa's text. He was so proud when I said I was planning to apply to University of Bristol and King's in London. He was happy because there was every chance I would stay in Bristol and live at home and commute. Meanwhile, I secretly knew that King's was my top choice. Meena once told me that Papa was desperate for there to be a lawyer in our family because of an incident when he was newly arrived in the country. He got hit by a car when he was cycling to work. And he lost so much money because he could not go anywhere while he was in a cast. Luckily, the couple in the house where he lodged took pity on him and put him in touch with their son, a barrister, who helped him bring a case to court and he got his lost earnings back. It was a small intervention but it was a needed one.

'This country only educates a few people to know how to use the system,' he said. 'The more of us there are, the more chance we have of using the system for good.'

He put the law on a pedestal. Everything became black and white. Mum once brought home a loaf of bread that she had accidentally forgotten to pay for. It remained in her shopping trolley when she loaded everything on to the conveyor belt. Papa marched us all back to the shop and got her to pay for it. The confused shop assistant took the 60p or whatever mostly because of his insistence, not because they cared. But to Papa, right was right.

And now his daughter was going to be on the right side of right.

If he knew where I was, instead of earning money for uni, he'd be so angry.

Jazz goes up first. He grabs the microphone off the stand. He paces, three steps to the left and three to the right, pretending to be working out what has annoyed him this week. His whole schtick is: 'We *should* complain about the little things because the big things are completely beyond our control. Here's a bunch of little things that annoy me.' I probably know his set off by heart.

I mouth along as he begins.

'Don't you hate it when people text you to ask if you saw their email?'

A few laughs. A few titters. Not me. I'm still at college. Jazz too. We have never texted anyone, 'Did you get my email?'.

'You don't have to reply to everything immediately. People used to write each other letters. And then send them. And then wait. Weeks, months, for a reply. No one was sending a carrier pigeon round with a note saying, "Did you receive my epistolary correspondence?".'

People laugh.

He ends on his big joke about his mum FaceTiming him from her bikini wax once. The face she pulls. Oh, ha ha ha, the weirdness of a teenage boy talking about women getting their legs waxed; the ability to contort his face, normally so serious, into something ridiculous. It shouldn't work. But it does.

A few other comics go onstage and I tune them out. I listen to my set on my earphones, practised in front of the bathroom mirror when everyone else was at work, and I try to centre myself. I've accidentally wandered into a battle royale with a banana I'm pretending is a gun. I'm not meant to be here. Maybe I am meant to be here. Maybe this is my goddamn origin story.

I'm staring at a text from Papa asking what I'm up to and when I'll be home, as Sam starts introducing the next act. I'm listening but not in the moment of it.

'Our next act describes herself as "*someone who came cos it was Thursday open-mic night, this is my first ever set please don't kill me* . . ." You heard her, folks. Please do not . . . under any circumstances . . . kill her. The one and only, for the first time, Madhu Krishna!'

The light applause sucks me into the room, and I realise that

Madhu Krishna is me. I run towards the stage like I just ran in late, and when I grab the mic people are laughing at me. I realise I've left my earphones in. Whoopsy poopsies. I whip them out and then do that awkward tuck into my tight jeans thing, leaving the entire length of one of the white wires dangling down to the floor. I then remember the jumper, and I put it on. TOKEN. People laugh. One person whoops.

I smile to the back of the room. Then I smile in Leila's direction. Then . . . I . . . bow.

I have no idea why. Everything in me feels fizzy. Like when you pour out a shaken bottle of Coke and it's still in *tssss* mode after a few minutes. Each bubble taking its turn to pop into the abyss.

I realise that from up here you can't actually see anyone. I cannot see the crowd. Or the compère. Or even Leila. The spotlight is that white. It's a bit of a blessing. Because all time has stopped. Everything has slowed down. All I can see is the bright light, literally like it's the end-of-life tunnel. And all I can hear is the gulp in my throat, the chap-chap-chap of my dry mouth and the quarry of my empty brain.

I bow again.

A few more laughs.

So I smile broadly. Trying to remember my first line. Once I know the first line, the muscle memory might kick in. But why can't I summon up the first line? What is wrong with me?

Come on, Madhu, what is it?

Something about my dad, about his weird impressions?

His weird expressions? Something. Something about . . . no . . . wait. The more I try to think about the line, the more I panic because I'm not saying anything and the more I'm not saying anything, the more I'm wasting my five minutes. I try to visualise a page of my notebook. All the words are blurred.

There's one laugh. A nervous one. Begging me to say something. Anything. The light is blinding and my mouth is dry and I have no idea what I'm doing up here. This time next year I'll be doing a law degree and my life, inevitably, will be over and I just can't be here. I cannot be here. I can't be here, I can't. This is useless. I am useless.

'Come on then,' someone shouts.

And I drop the microphone. I just drop it on the floor. It clunks and does that feedback wail you only really hear in the movies.

In the ensuing silence, I realise I have no option but to run, to get off the stage, to just go. But my body is frozen to the spot. I cannot move . . . anything. Not my brain, my hands, my feet. I am just stuck. I ball my fists, which feels like progress. People are laughing, like this is part of the performance. *Maybe I should just pick the mic up and replace it on the stand and shout 'thank you very much', like it was meant to be* . . . is what I think now I could have done, but we're not in the bit where I'm telling you how I got here, we're in the moment of the biggest humiliation my life has ever experienced.

I have failed.

I feel something push past me, bending as it goes. I realise it's Sam, arriving onstage, picking up the dropped microphone and placing it on the stand. He clenches his clipboard under his arm and applauds me.

Which is just the worst bit. I'm being applauded for failing.

So I run. I run off the stage, grabbing my backpack from the stairs, and I head for the door. I don't even hear what Sam says that garners such a huge laugh. All I know is that it's at my expense.

I'm a failure.

3

The worst thing about getting older is when you play the 'I'm a teenager' card. Like, on the one hand, cheap bus fare please. On the other, what do you mean I can't rent a car and go to a drive-in and watch the new Human Centipede *movie?*

It needs a better punchline. Sadly, the punchline to my entire stand-up career is that it started and finished in the same set that started and finished in the same minute, so rather than finish the routine I started about dognostics, I'm binning my notebooks. Time to focus on the rest of my life. The dream is dead.

Papa knocks on my door. I know it's him and not Mum because, well, he knocks. She just opens the door, hand over her eyes, shouting, 'You busy?'

'Come in, Papa,' I say.

The door opens and there he stands in his jabba lehenga. White and thigh-length.

'It could have been someone else,' he says.

'Who? The postman?'

'OK, joker. How was the pizza place?'

My cheeks prickle with my obfuscation from last night. I've

been so focused on doing that set that I forgot I lied to him. I told him I was working.

Papa notices my laptop screen and grins when he sees that I'm doing some budgeting scenarios for uni. I've budgeted £0 for fun. That sounds about right. The thing is, paying for halls, paying for books, paying for all of the privilege of being at uni is . . . a *lot*. And when you got a shop-owner dad who works seven days a week just to scrape by . . . you have to be able to take that burden off him. Have to, right? I'm hoping I end up going to uni in Bristol, because that'll take some costs down and I can keep my pizza job.

Asian parents know the hustle. They work their arses off. Tell you about their sacrifice. Push you to an earner of a job. And then mentally move into your spare room before you've even earned your first paycheque.

My dad knows that if I'm a lawyer, he's got a bapuji flat ready to go. I can take him and my mum away from all this.

At least now we don't live above the shop any more. It means living in a flat where we're still on top of each other, but at least the shop's a bus ride away so I don't have to do the odd shift when Papa needs a sleep or a poop.

Life feels dimmer in the days after my disastrous stand-up crash and burn. It's now Sunday and I'm eating breakfast at the kitchen table with my textbooks in front of me. This is me now. Be good enough to get that law degree. The vision I had for the rest of my life is over.

Yesterday was a blur. I ignored texts from Leila, I ignored my parents' bickering, I even ignored whatever I was watching on Netflix and I mourned the end of my dreams. And I mourned the tragedy of being seventeen and feeling like I blew my only chance at happiness. And then I thought, *I wonder if I'll still feel this way when I'm older*, and then I cried at the prospect of getting older. And when I texted my friend Sunny to find out when he's back from his training camp in London and he sent me a photo of a guy he was going on a date with, I cried because I couldn't even really cuss this guy to his face for looking so happy.

Before I knew it, it was dinner time and I took a bowl of dhal to my bedroom and I didn't eat it. Papa had the IPL on full blast through my floorboards. And I fell asleep, not realising how tired you can get spending the whole day in the same room, crying. Like, it's legit more exhausting than running a marathon in the tiredness stakes.

At least today I have a shift at the restaurant to look forward to. I'm trying to do as many shifts as I can this year; to earn enough money to not be a burden any more. Earn money to maybe take myself off to Edinburgh one summer. Be a fan. A superfan. The biggest fan. A fan of the funny people. Because alas, I am not one of the funny people.

Self-pity, you never let me down.

Self-pity leads me to listen to my favourite Kareena Patel album on the bus as I head to work. I ripped it from her YouTube channel and converted it to an mp3 so I could listen whenever I want. I can mouth it word for word. I'm so good I know her timing, intonation and vocal ticks where she paces out for where a laugh should be.

Self-pity makes me cry instead of laughing.

Self-pity makes me buy a bubble tea at the spot across the road from the pizza place so I can sort my face out before going in. No one needs to know I've been crying on the inside so much my face looks like it's been suppressing a fart since dawn.

Self-pity means thinking I need to do something nice for someone else so when I stop at the shop to grab a sandwich for lunch, I ask the homeless guy if he wants anything.

'Cider,' he replies, appreciatively.

What do I do here? I have to make a choice: do I say no, due to some well-meaning but patronising concern for his welfare, or because it is a few quid more than I was willing to spend, or because I'm seventeen and barely try to buy alcohol for myself, so why would I risk humiliation and trouble for this guy? All of this flashes through my head, as I react to the word 'cider'.

'Sir, I am seventeen!' I finally shout, and walk into the shop.

'Sir?' I hear him say, rolling it around his tongue like he has never been treated with such fake respect before.

Self-pity means this interaction is going to bother me all damn day.

'Crisps then,' he shouts after me. 'Salt and vinegar.'

I turn around and give him a thumbs up and he just shakes his head at me.

My shift is busy. Which is what you want. If a place is slow the boss makes you clean, otherwise you're just being paid to stand around and play Netflix Top Trumps.

Did you see . . .?

I'm on season one, episode seven.

Wait till you get to season two.

I can't believe what happens in season three . . .

Did you know that [actor's name] was in [another show] with [another actor]?

Yeah, of course I knew them from that. Have you seen them in . . .?

My head is filled with regrets so I want the tables to be full, and to have a queue of people, a mixture of large groups and small, a cavalcade of dude-bros who think aggressive piss-taking is a perfectly normal way to flirt, and families where the parents just want to eat their pizza and sink their pints in peace while the kids either run around, chuck food on the floor or allow themselves to be pacified by a device of some sort. Occasionally, you get a cute old couple, British fogies who've never tried this 'foreign stuff' before and, actually, cheese and tomato on dough is delicious, or it's old Italian couples who love the history of this place and knew Danny's dad. Sometimes you just get pengers on a date, and you know they'll last, because this is far from a flashy or cool place. It's always popping, and it's always full and it's one of those 'if you know you know' spots. And that is why I love working here.

Today, Jazz decides to take a table all by himself in my station.

I don't recognise him at first because he's not wearing his stage gear. He's wearing a plain white T-shirt and chinos. His hair seems freer, less stylised and slicked down. He has a notebook in front of him.

I leave him waiting long enough for Danny to point him out to me. When I roll my eyes, Danny asks if I know him.

'Sadly, yes,' I say.

'Want me to ask him to leave?' Danny asks. For all his faults, he is good on ridding the restaurant of creepy men. Once, he 86ed someone who tried to upskirt a customer at another table. Even called the police on him. Another time, he interrupted a date that was going badly to ask the other guy if he needed Danny to call him a taxi home. When the aggressive date reacted badly and threw a wine glass on the floor, Danny grabbed him into an arm lock and pulled him out of the restaurant.

'I'm good,' I say. 'I don't know him *know him*, it's just weird he's here. He's harmless. I'm fine.'

Danny nods, not believing a word of what I'm saying to him.

I approach Jazz tentatively. As I do, something awkward about the way I'm looking at him makes him open the book to a random page and point at it.

'Hey,' I say, with a smile the size of my face, stretching out what I think are the tennis ball-sized bags under my eyes. 'What can I get you? Something to drink?'

'Oh, right, yeah,' he says, ruffling the back of his head and closing his eyes as if deep in thought. The pageantry of this scene makes me want to laugh. 'Water, please.'

'Still or sparkling?'

'Just tap,' he murmurs.

'Government juice? Got it.'

'What's government juice?' he asks.

'Oh, it's what my dad calls tap water. He jokes about MI5 putting weird trackers in it all the time and the NHS filling our taps with some form of hallucinogen to keep us all angry but not really angry.'

'Your dad's a conspiracy theorist?'

'Yeah, and not a cheap one. That's why he has his water bottled. And anything to eat?'

'Oh, right, yeah. Um, what's good here?' he asks. Again with the hair ruffle. I look down at his notebook. Probably filled with jokes and all, knowing him.

'I hear the pizza's nice,' I reply, looking around the room, noticing Danny seating a couple, and their kid, in my station. I recognise the dad as coming in a few weeks ago with just the kid and me trying to work out if he was a weekend dad or a treating dad or just a dad on a Sunday. Now with this woman, who seems like she'd rather be at home asleep, I'm not so sure.

'Pizza, what's that? Like hot cheese and tomato on flatbread? Isn't that just Italian . . .'

'Is this a bit?' I ask Jazz and he grabs his hands in front of him, on the table, like he's been told off. Which he has. 'I'm busy, Jazz. Do you need a few minutes?'

I head over to the couple to take their drinks order, wait for them to deliberate on whether to have a boozy drink or not, which feels like a tense argument about who's driving home, take the order over to the bar to sort before returning to them for their pizza order and then to Jazz.

'So?'

'I want to help you,' he asks.

'Tip generously then. And order something expensive. The lobster of pizzas maybe.'

'With stand-up,' he murmurs.

'I think you have me confused with someone else,' I say.

'I know you could be good,' he says.

'Oh, is it? When would you have worked that out? From all the time you've spent not talking to me? From all the time I've been onstage and you've wet yourself laughing? From our deep and meaningful friendship where you know exactly who I am and what I'm about?'

'Leila played me your practice voice memo,' he says.

I look over at Danny, who crosses the restaurant with the swiftness.

'I'm sorry,' Danny says. 'I need to ask you to leave.'

Danny holds the door open for me, as he does with all of us when we finish our shift.

He spies Jazz, persistent, get-the-message-please saviour Jazz, sitting on a bollard outside the shop, writing in his notebook. Jazz looks at me and stands up, nervously. Danny leans in close and quietly asks if I'm OK. I nod.

'Yeah, I can mess him up no problem,' I say. 'Look at him perching. I could clothesline him into the path of a bus with no fuss.'

'I'd pay to see that,' Danny says. 'By the way, you were really friendly tonight. Everyone complimented your good energy, thank you.'

He likes to leave us with a compliment about our shift, even if it went horrendously, just because he's a nice guy who likes to have staff who don't mind this being the place they earn money at. He's under no illusion that in this part of the city, in this type of restaurant, serving this type of food, at these types of prices, the clientele and the staff will always be in transit.

I smile and head out on to the street. Jazz stands, ruining the opportunity I had to surge forward and push him backwards.

'This is not creepy behaviour at all,' I say. 'What's next? Writing me notes using your blood as ink?'

'Look, Leila kept going on about how good you were, and look, I was sceptical. I saw you bottle it, after all. And she said she had this recording of you and I was like, prove it, and she played it, and there was a couple of good things . . .'

'Right,' I say, my brain processing all this. 'Tell me more nice things about myself.'

'I think your delivery is good, confident, you have some really

37

perfect one-liners and the world you build is sweet and funny. I could have done with a few more killer punch lines. Where you dig in deep.'

I stop walking and face him. He has his hands in his pockets, like he's just given me an encouraging locker-room pep talk, one foot up on the bench as he dips towards me.

'Listen, coach, I didn't ask you to do any of this, OK?'

'I know. I'm just trying to help,' Jazz says, his voice less confident now, wavering like a guy who's just realised this jelly bath is actually a viper's nest.

'Bruv, I ain't standing here trying to be a stand-up. I had a go. It didn't go. So I go to work and I go to college and I will just do what I need to do, feel me?'

'I feel you.'

'You could help me write my university application form if you want? I definitely need help with that.'

I don't check to see if Jazz accepts this challenge or not because my bus is approaching my stop so I spring into what I'd love to call a sprint, but is actually just Clompy McGee clomping in the direction of a big vehicle.

As I sit down on the top deck, I watch him, watching me from the street.

4

College has this smell, right? It's the smell of teachers' frustration. Instant coffee and stale fish sandwiches. It's more oppressive the earlier in the day you arrive because the stench of Lynx Africa masks it once all the dudes arrive.

I'm here early to write my personal statement for the university application. In my head, it's titled, 'Why I'm doing a law degree, I guess love me love me let me in so Papa doesn't think I'm a disappointment like his other daughter, the estranged one'. Bit on the nose. I'll probably just call it, 'I am the law'.

I couldn't possibly write it at home. A personal statement at home would end up being a depressed confessional about my life expectations being crushed before they even got started and me having to settle for this stupid career that the television shows all make look glamorous with expensive offices and power suits and scouring through small print in contracts so you can ask just one more question at the right minute.

Being a lawyer. Cripes. What a nightmare. What a lucrative nightmare.

Thing is, I'm good with tunnel vision. I reckon I'd be a badass at it and I could earn enough money to buy Mum and Papa somewhere to live. And maybe even buy the shop off them and hire someone else to run it and make their lives easier. Kareena Patel did something similar. She went to law school and spent her days in lectures and the library, and she gigged every single night. I'm not saying that's the path for me right now, but my god, I am glad my hero chose this.

I sit in front of a computer and stare at the accusatory blinking cursor for a good hour until the shuffle of teenage bodies around me reminds me that we have things to do.

I float through history. I half-listen in politics. I keep myself to myself. I am quiet. I speak to no one, I am still in mourning.

Shanai asks me to lunch after our politics class and I go with her. Luckily she is one of those friends who can fill a silence on your off days. She doesn't mind. She just likes talking. Usually, I am more than happy to jibber jabber with her about nothing in particular. Today, between Jazz and the impending deadline of the wordless personal statement, I have nothing in the tank.

We sit and I watch the world and Shanai scroll through her phone, occasionally pointing TikToks at me.

I think I'm angry. I think that's what I'm feeling. Not sadness or grief or remorse. Like, a deep bubbling anger. Mainly at myself. Isn't this the process of acceptance? I'm angry that I blew my moment. There could be other moments, a lifetime of moments, but this was *the* moment. Moments are limited. Moments are conditional.

I want to point my rage at something more useful than just myself.

The canteen is buzzing. I have a sandwich in my bag but it's too sad and I don't want to eat something that feels as bland and uninspiring and depressed as I'm feeling. Nothing announces that you don't care about yourself any more than a sandwich. A sandwich says, *I will be what my colonisers want me to be.* I almost reach for my notebook to write this down as a brilliant bit about sandwiches, but then I remember I am stand-up no more, and my notebooks are in the bin. Not even the recycling bin. They are headed for landfill.

The menu in the canteen is no better. Shanai orders the jerk chicken and snickers when I roll my eyes.

'Look,' she says, laughing, her fingers pointing at me, acrylics glinting in the harsh school lights. 'I know it'll be gross. But it's better than a sandwich.'

'Yeah, nothing to remind us more of the impact of colonialism than stale sandwiches and spiceless versions of our ancestors' food,' I say. 'And look, today all I need is some vegetables. I think they'll give me the vim I need to complete this godforsaken day.'

'Broccoli ain't going to save you,' Shanai says.

'From my personality? Probably not, but at least my skin will be glowing.'

I must say it loud enough for others to hear because people around me laugh and the person serving shakes their head, like, *Come on mate, my job's hard enough without you ungrateful teens giving me a hard time and all.*

I hold a hand up to apologise and order nothing, consigning

myself to the cold sandwich Papa made for the entire household. Since Meena left, our packed lunches have been the same thing every day. Say what you will about my estranged sister, and believe me, they all do. But she cared about our lunches and would go to the effort of making elaborate salads, interesting flatbread fillings, the occasional falafel, sometimes a bowl of pawa, other times, leftovers with salad. She'd be up early most days to do it, and if she knew she was gonna need some time in bed because of whatever she was doing, she pre-made things before she went out that night, and they were never meals that would go soggy in the fridge. She was a don like that. I miss her.

Kareena Patel has this joke about how siblings are proof that you are capable of human emotion. Because you will feel at least one thing towards them at all times.

Shanai and I sit at a table by ourselves. She looks around the room.

'What's going on with Marvin?' I ask, knowing that she's scanning for him. She looks at me all weird, like I can see her thoughts.

I mean, it's not a hard leap to make.

'He texted me to break up,' Shanai says, sighing, a rumble of tears not far from the surface.

'He texted you?'

'Yeah,' she says.

'To break up?'

'Yeah.'

'Stone. Cold.'

She picks her phone up off the table and finds the text, showing me. Marvin is attempting to be magnanimous but is actually coming off as mean and stupid.

'He doesn't want to be tied down so young – what does that mean?' I ask.

'He wants to date other people.'

'Why doesn't he say that?' I respond. 'Why does he have to make it seem like you're the one tying him down and he wants to be a free bird, soaring high?'

'But then he's like, we're destined to be together, why worry about right now?'

'You mean, "Please can I have permission to mess around with as many girls as I want now? Don't worry, I'll marry you later"?'

'Exactly.'

'Exactly.'

Shanai is furious. I'm mad for her. What an absolutely horrific way to break up with someone.

I spy Marvin on the other side of the canteen. He sits at a table, holding court with a large group of people. He has his arm around a girl. I can't see who – she is engulfed in his badboy Raiders jacket that I covet so.

'You OK?'

'No,' Shanai says, spooning the jerk chicken into her mouth. 'This is disgusting. Spiceless mess on a dry chicken.'

'And the food's gross too,' I add, smiling like a poster for an

Edinburgh show. It doesn't get the reaction I want. 'Who's he with, anyway?'

Shanai stands up and walks over to Marvin's table. I go to follow her but she holds up a hand to say she's fine. So I let her go and sit back down and look at my sandwich.

I want to bin it. It smells and tastes like it was made days ago, by someone who despises me. I resolve to eat it quickly, in four bites. The first one is so dry, I want to spit it out on to the table. But I'm in company and besides, if I saw that kind of behaviour from someone else, I'd want to vomit down their back.

When Shanai comes back, she tells me she's fine quickly and assertively before I even speak, which is a sure-fire way of telling me she is not fine. When I see a tear fall on her sad tasteless rubber jerk chicken, I stand up.

There is no way this idiot is treating my friend like this.

'What did he say?' I ask.

'Leave it,' she replies. 'He is cruel.'

'Sorry, babe,' I say. 'I cannot leave it.'

I cross the canteen, mouth loaded, settings on 'execution'.

'Madhu,' Shanai calls after me. I know she's hesitating, wondering whether to follow me or sit with the chicken. I'm on autopilot now. This guy needs to know he is an idiot. And I am the best person to tell him this very thing.

'Marvin,' I say, as I approach. Marvin turns to me and I see the girl's face, the one he's with.

Oh no. It's Pri. From the trainer place. I suddenly feel bad.

I assured Shanai this would not happen. Dammit. No wonder Shanai is so upset.

'Marvin,' I say. He smiles, first with embarrassment and then with a feigned confidence, like he's trying to own the situation he has just been caught in.

'Madhu,' he says. He extends a fist to spud. I look at it.

'Marvin, what's wrong with men? I only ask because you seem like an everyman here. I said to you months ago, yes, all men, and you argued, not all men. And yet here you are, being a man. Like your girlfriend – who is sitting over there wishing I wasn't standing over you telling you what's what – doesn't exist.'

'Ex-girlfriend.'

'And why did you break up, Marvin?' I say, circling the table, still on autopilot.

'I know, I know,' he says, hugging Pri in further. 'Love is mysterious, that's all I'll say.' All Pri's body language points to her wanting to run out of the canteen and head for the hills, live out the rest of her days off-grid, believing conspiracy theories and hunting bears in the Somerset countryside. 'But it's like, if we're not together, and this is exactly why she thought we should break up, I might as well do it,' he adds.

'Thanks,' Pri murmurs, like, *Wow Marv, such a romantic.*

'So there was no crossover?' I say, looking at Pri, who gets her phone out and starts checking it obsessively.

'It's like, what's the point of expecting the bare minimum from human beings these days, right?' I announce to the table.

'The thing is, Marvin, I think you're stupid. Stupid because you had a brilliant girlfriend, and stupid because you assume her insecurities were annoying but you might as well take advantage, and stupid because you didn't, for one second, think about her. You're so stupid, dude. You think Santa's real, probably. Spoiler alert, it's just your mum and dad. Also, you're nearly an adult, why do you have a stocking on Christmas Day? You're so stupid, I heard you once tried to drown a fish. Shanai once told me that you like to lay your clothes out before putting them on and give them a little pep talk about the day. Is that true? Pri, honestly, you could do better. Marvin once got locked in his own car, and the keys were in his hand. Shanai and I once had to explain the plot of *Paddington Bear* to him. He definitely is not worth your time . . .'

I realise that people are filming my rant and it makes me stumble over my words for a second. Suddenly visible, even though I'm literally shouting down a fool in the school canteen at the height of lunchtime. Shanai has moved towards us, arms folded, watching me. I lock eyes with her and she flashes me the quickest, most appreciative smile. She won't have liked me making her business hot, particularly, but she is probably enjoying the dressing down I'm giving Marvin.

'One of the advantages of not going out with Shanai is I don't have to hang out with you any more, I guess,' Marvin says, laughing into silence.

'My point, dear little one, is, imagine being this boring. Imagine being this predictable. Imagine being this much of a stereotype that I can read you like this in front of everyone and you can look at your hands and your lunch detritus and feel a small amount of embarrassment but also the creeping sadness that, my god, she's right, you know. What a disappointment I am. When you go home tonight, and you look at yourself in the mirror before you go to bed and you weigh up whether tonight you should brush your teeth or not, all I'm going to say is, always brush your teeth. Always. Because when all is said and done in years to come and you realise what an utterly disappointing, crushingly boring stereotype you are, at least you'll have nice teeth.'

The table erupts in laughter. It's a happy, gleeful, appreciative laughter. I have just taken down the head of the pride. And I'm the over-talkative cartoon mouse. The mouse took on the lion and now the lion is standing up, grabbing his tray and pushing past me, whispering a curse word in my direction as he shoulder barges me out of the way. The laughter echoes in his wake as he tries to get out of its blast radius. The table has a healthy mix of big high-pitched hyena flurries and deep, bassy defined 'ha's. It has middling laughs that fill out the frequencies. I bow to the camera phones, awkward, not sure why they're filming this dragging and I turn and grab Shanai, practically running out of the canteen, leaving my stale sandwich behind.

I allow myself a smile as I look back to watch Marvin stomp out of the entrance on the other side of the canteen. I did good. I smashed that set.

Shanai buys me a sweet treat as a thank you and we sit

under the stairs leading to the English department, which is a big no-no, and we eat them. Mine is an elaborate passionfruit, mango and lime Mexican paleta. My favourite. For special occasions only. Shanai has a cone with a flake. It may be cold outside, and cold in our hearts, but it's colder on our tongues.

'You're funny,' Shanai says.

'I know,' I reply, winking at her over the top of my paleta.

'Seriously, you should think about doing stand-up or something,' she adds.

'Yeah, maybe,' I reply.

Only Leila knows about my aborted attempt to get on the mic.

'Thank you,' Shanai says. 'I didn't know I needed that. I mean, when you started rinsing him, I thought I was going to die.'

'Thanks,' I say.

I feel my pocket vibrating and grab my phone. It's Meena, my sister. She hasn't called me since . . . I don't know when. Not for weeks. I answer it in case it's an emergency.

'Hello?'

The phone clicks off and the call is ended. Worried, I call her back and it immediately goes to voicemail.

'Butt dial?' Shanai asks.

'I guess,' I reply.

'Listen, the way you rinsed Marvin got me creasing,' Shanai says, laughing as I dry out my paleta stick of all its remaining syrup. 'Honestly, your tongue is vicious. I never want to get on the wrong side of you.'

I point the paleta stick at her. 'Don't you mess with me, kid, I'll take you out,' I say.

I don't feel what she's feeling. I don't like my anger being the thing that makes people laugh. It's so easy to be dismissed as the angry brown person. It's so easy for a vicious tongue to create power imbalances. Like, if I make an idiot as Marvin feel small by rinsing him, and everyone laughs at him, there I am throwing the weak to the hyenas, cackling as they feed on his body, knowing I am the one who fed them. I don't like it. But everyone loves it. And I love that they love it.

Meena used to be my one. If I could make her laugh, I knew I had done good. She is the type of audience who says, 'that's funny' to a joke. Like she objectively knows it's funny but it hasn't been strong enough to elicit an eruption from her. One that bypasses all neurons and synapses, all brain function and goes for the marrow of her funny bone, making her crease.

Imagine, me cracking a joke about something, making an observation about Papa and Mum or someone at the bus stop or some mad thing white people/men do, and her nodding and going, that's funny.

It's disheartening. Because what you want is the . . . I don't know what to call it really, so I'll just mislabel it 'the thing'. The thing when someone's face creases and that laugh rises up out of the core of them.

I remember once Meena and I having that moment.

We were stuck on a ferry, in the back of the car. It was the end of a disastrous weekend on the Isle of Wight and we were tired. We're an Asian family; we rarely take any holiday, since it means closing the shop.

Of course it rained the one time we did. It was summer in the UK. When you need the weather to be reliable, it cuts its thumb at you and rolls its eyes. Honestly, this country is so contrary, even its weather system is like, you want to enjoy yourselves? Nah, don't think so. The English would rather have a miserable time so they can moan about it in the pub than just run through a muddy field barefoot and experience life. My god. Just shut up and enjoy it.

Anyway, it rained. And when I say it rained, I know you're imagining a thorough amount of rain. I want you to double that and not imagine monsoons because, sadly, British weather is never as dramatic, or as beautiful, or as cleansing as a monsoon. I want you to imagine the type of incessant drizzle that soaks you to your core.

Needless to say, we had a miserable time. Papa lost his wallet, Mum had catered for every meal with a cool box of plastic containers, with theplas and shaaks and a box of browning lettuce, meaning the only meal we had out was a soggy fish and chips on the beach.

And Meena and I just couldn't keep it together. It was so typical. And so hilarious. And so hilariously typical. That every little thing that went wrong sent us into a sore-throated cough-laugh, like the well of joy at our collective misery was running dry.

The ferry back was a relief.

Because the weather was such a madness, we were instructed to remain in our cars, and so we did for the choppy return trip.

I needed to raise everyone's spirits. I had been staring at a dog in the car next to us. It looked just like a teddy bear. It was precious and small and fluffy and cuddly, with round ears and a hug me hug me hug me face. It was so cute it managed to evade my dognostic filtration system.

'It looks like a teddy dog,' I said to Meena, who was resting her head on my shoulder, staring at her phone. She looked up and smiled.

'Wow,' she said. 'It really does.'

Mum looked over, and so did Papa and suddenly the lone wolf at the wheel of the car felt that she had the gaze of four inquisitive browns. She bowed her head at her phone.

I erupted in a confident funk-and-soul yell, 'He's just a fluffy teddy do-oh-og. He's a teddy dog teddy dog (teddy dog!), he's just a lovely teddy do-oh-og . . .' Obviously, the backing vocals were in falsetto and sounded like they were stabbing the music in the face.

Meena lost it. She lost it so badly that she said she weed a little, which made me need the toilet. Watching her double over into the centre of the car, and all of us looking at her and laughing at how funny she found this dumb song, that was a precious moment we'll never get back.

That day feels like a long time ago as I stand here looking at Meena's name on my missed call list.

I text to ask if she's OK. It goes to 'read' and I see the reply bubbles start up, then go, then start up again, all while Shanai is telling me about Hannah Gadsby's Netflix special like I'm a comedy noob.

5

I don't know who uploaded the video. And I don't really see the online reaction because I'm not really on the apps. And I don't really understand the impact of 'going viral'. And I don't even know why no one thought to ask my permission. And I don't know why me cussing out my friend's boyfriend warrants any attention beyond the people that know us. But it happens.

That afternoon, I feel hypervisible. Like, is this how quickly this stuff works? Walking out of college, I can hear snippets of my voice on people's phones. I don't know if they connect the me walking past them to the me in the video. I sit on the bus and I hear myself out of their speakers. I feel people looking at me and then down at their phone screens. I get two thumbs up from two separate people, I get a nod of appreciation (although it could also be the minority solidarity head-nod), I even get spudded by a random as I get off the bus.

I look up to see Marvin through the top deck window, and we make eye contact. And I mouth 'sorry' at him and he waves it off to say he's fine.

Which I don't get. If I was that obliterated and then it became a viral video in our college, then I would be revenge-seeking.

Maybe the revenge he seeks will involve a plan to regain my trust and get close to me so that when the knife slides in cleanly between my ribs, he and I are sharing an in-joke about something and I don't see it coming.

Maybe, even, he messed up, got caught messing up and the visibility of his messing up has made him re-evaluate his actions. Maybe I have shamed him into being a better person. Or maybe it's not that deep.

Either way, I'm glad he's not mad at me.

Not that it matters. I guess, it's more like, dude's popular. I wouldn't want to engage with what it feels like to be on the wrong side of that, particularly.

Either way, he's an idiot for what he did to Shanai.

At home, I sign up for a Twitter account. I'm going to have to find this video, I guess, and see what is going on. I've never seen the point of social media for someone like me. I suppose it'd be a good place to follow comedians and see how they hone their craft and maybe even engage them in chat. But about what?

Once I have my profile, which is just my name (why are there no other Madhu Krishnas on Twitter?), I search for the video. I find it quickly because someone from college has responded 'Madhu Krishna YOU LEGEND' to the original tweet. Plus, it has generated a hashtag.

#poorMarvin

My gift to the world.

Oh god.

I cannot bring myself to watch the video until the end. It autoplays all over my timeline. I click on the hashtag and try to scroll through but it's just the same video, on repeat. It's too much. Seeing your face again and again. And seeing people either loving you or hating you. No in between. Loads of great supportive tweets by women of colour all calling me hilarious and brilliant. Loads of hateful tweets by all the Dave4934800s of the internet calling me smug and unfunny, entitled and loud. Basically, sit down, leave the poor man alone. How dare you speak up? Who the hell are you?

I have been on Twitter barely an hour when people start tagging my account into their tweets about the video. How did they find me so quickly? As an experiment, I start typing @madhukrishna into Twitter and my profile comes up right at the top. I throw my phone on the bed and head downstairs to get away from the noise.

Papa is watching the news so I sit with him, commenting on the local reporter's hair, suddenly much less grey than it was last week.

'Should I dye my hair?' Papa asks me.

'Definitely not,' I reply.

He runs his hands through his thinning grey locks.

'I want to look younger,' he says, quietly.

'For who?'

'For me, baby. For me.'

'I can help you invent a time machine if you want, Papa,'

I say and he rolls his eyes at me. He always makes it out like I'm so mean. 'You're perfect the way you are,' I add.

I try a few more conversation starters to keep me from looking at my phone, but it's like I can hear the vibrations of notifications through the walls, like the screen lighting up with people getting in touch is bright and covering the entire house in its spread.

Papa asks me a question about my day. I brush him off with a vague answer about things being fine and I walk out of the room, practically running back to my bedroom.

My pulse rate jolts when I see the phone. It's lit up with notifications. Sweet notifications. Feed-my-addiction notifications. I've-only-had-Twitter-for-an-hour-or-so notifications but I-need-you-to-inject-yourselves-directly-into-my-veins notifications.

I scroll through them. A lot are Twitter, a bunch are WhatsApp and then one, a text from a number I don't recognise, going, 'OMG KAREENA CO-SIGN? SICK.'

What.

What is happening?

I unlock the phone and hit Twitter. I am studious in my slow scrawl through my feed but I don't have to look hard to see it. It. The it. The only it. The everything.

Kareena Patel, the Patel, Kareena The Patel, my GD hero, has tagged me into a quote tweet of the video, and written, **Yes yes @madhukrishna, you hilarious individual. You remind me of a young me. How do I get you on my show?**

I drop the phone and look up.

The postcard of her I have next to my mirror stares back at me. I try to process this fact. This stone-cold fact.

Kareena Patel knows who I am.

What even is life.

She. Knows. Who. I. Am.

6

Kareena has a new season of a late-night show starting soon, called *Kareena Kareena*. They have put it on at a time where, if you're watching it live, you *really* want to be watching it. It's broadcast at a 'fans only' time.

What I feel when I see the billboard advertising the show at the end of Old Market is, *I knew about you before you were billboard-worthy*.

It's funny how fans get protective over people who they think belong to them. Like I would ever know how she feels about the world, whether she considers breakfast is the most important meal of the day, what she listens to as she walks to work and who she's in a text chain with about something utterly dumb.

We don't know these people and yet, the way she watches over me when I sleep from her postcard's vantage point; the way her albums are a comfort listen or watch for me; the way my first attempt at stand-up was learning her 'cat person' routine word by word, pause by pause, gesture by gesture; the way I just know her, it's enough to understand why I am so protective about this sister.

I remember going to see her do a club set last year. Which was rare. She doesn't usually do club sets and why on earth would she travel halfway across the country for a fifteen-minute set on a Saturday night dealing with heckling stag dos, at her level. It was so bonkers I had to go see it. I went by myself.

I looked to my left at one point, into the aisle, and there she was, standing next to me, fingers around her chin, thinking. She was so still, so straight and poised, so in whatever zone she was in.

And then she went up. And by god, my god, by god, by Jove, my god, she was Destructor the Obscene, that's how good she was; so good I just invented a supervillain alter ego for her, cos no other will do her justice. She killed the mic dead. She sprayed shots into the crowd and absolutely crushed them all. She announced she wasn't going to bother with her intended set tonight; she had wanted to try some jokes out. But first, she needed to set the record straight, especially seeing as there were only two brown people in the room; she pointed to me in the darkness and my heart flinched at the fact that she had seen me, and she led us on a hilarious alternative history of the word 'woke' and how it had been stolen by white people to mean, I don't like all this equality chat so I'm gonna call you woke as a slur and strip it of its original meaning. Points were made. And the crowd was mostly silent.

Except me. And she kept referring to the audience of one she had tonight, which was the only other brown girl here because she needed me to leave the club knowing a better world was possible. And the rest of the audience could suck its mum.

She fought them all. It was like watching a game of chess boxing – one second she was throwing out jabs and hooks and uppercuts and the next it was knight to king's rook and trap the queen in a corner.

She bounded off stage and bounced. As she passed me, she put a hand on my shoulder and lightly tapped it.

'They're all idiots,' she said.

She left.

But it was enough. A heroic act to prove exactly why I loved her so much. I stare again at what she has written.

People are quote tweeting it, retweeting it, commenting under it – a mixture of agreement about how amazing I am, and more things about what an idiot I am.

Kareena must have time because she is calling out all the people cussing me with sexist or racist dog-whistles, telling them what they're really saying, exposing the insidious underbelly.

It's amazing to watch.

Then she follows me.

So I immediately follow her.

And so then, here we are, both following each other on the bird app. Kareena rating my video, me sitting here in confusion about whether to join in or bask in the fact that my life's hero is going to bat for me. Defending me against people who are finding this video terrible, like the worst thing they have ever seen, like I'm some sort of war criminal bad person.

Maybe I do like this app.

Do I send her a message? Oh god, wait, can I send her a message? What's that quote from *Jurassic Park*? Just because you can do something, probably doesn't mean you should, right?

Should I be cool? I've never really met anyone famous before. The closest was Hari, the boxer dude that took Sunny under his wing. But he's from round here and we went to the same college and so that doesn't really feel like someone famous. Besides, you can't really compare him with . . . Kareena. The queen of stand-up. The person who made it OK to do stand-up about stuff that wasn't just funny Indian accents and stereotype-confirming.

Look, I know what you're thinking, dear friend, this isn't the place to make our big political points. Just tell me if you DMed her or not.

I'm stalling because I'd rather tell you all this than the bizarre versions of messages that I edited in my head. Should I tell her how much she means to me? Or should I be all cool and go safe for the 'follow celebrity, now let me show you how it's done'? Or should I just tell her she's well funny? Or is that patronising? Or just thank her for the follow like I'm a small business trying to build a solid customer base?

None of these work.

Because while I am drafting the DM, I see the bubbles of her typing ellipsis appear. And I'm so shocked, I drop my phone.

And because it lands on its front, the last thing I typed, as I grabbed on to it, before it slipped out of my hands properly, was **fwehfoajh** and the floor shamed me, by hitting send.

Yup, my first communication with my hero is **fwehfoajh**.

She stops typing.

I stare at the phone and then I try to delete **fwehfoajh**. But you can't delete DMs for some reason. Twitter, why do you hate me?

Fwehfoajh

Fwehfoajh

Then, the bubbles start up again.

And she writes, **Is that French for what's up? I got a F at GCSE and that.**

I laugh at her generosity. Thank god she's not making me feel like a complete idiot.

It's actually Gujarati for 'welcome to my world', I reply.

That's not true. I'm Gujarati. We don't welcome just anyone to our world. Not until they've taken their shoes off and brought the jellabee.

LOL, I reply.

LOL? What on earth is wrong with me? LOL? LOL! *LOL*, she says. It's excruciating, trying to have a dialogue with your absolute hero like you're both normal human beings. Because neither of you are. She's a celebrity. And you're a nobody. Worse than that, a viral nobody.

I start typing out such a reply, telling her how much she

means to me. And then she writes, **Your video made me crease. Who is your rep? I need you on my show**.

I drop the phone again.

Please no fwehfoajh this time.

I run around the flat. Mum and Papa are on a call with my auntie in India in the kitchen so I run into every room except that one and I do a circuit and I come back out. I don't go in Meena's room because no one has been in Meena's room since the day after she left. Papa went in and put everything she didn't take into a box and left it in her wardrobe. Mum cleaned the room, stoically. I stood in the doorway and ran through all the memories I had of being in that room. Lying on the bed doing impressions of our parents, listening quietly as Meena told me about friend woes, sitting cross legged on the bed playing her boyfriend's Switch while they studied on the floor.

It feels like a broken bone in an otherwise functioning ecosystem.

It's only distracting for a fragment before I remember . . . Kaaaareeeeeenaaaaaa Patellllllll! Ridiculous.

I remember, I have to preserve the momentum of our conversation so I throw myself on to the sofa and think of a reply.

Rep? I reply. **Fam, I'm 17.** I think I sound cute.

OK we need to fix that, you need a rep superstar. I can help you with that. First thing is, get you to the studio, have a coffee and get you on my show.

I want to drop the phone again. I want to throw it out of the window. I'd need to open the window first because broken glass in this carpet is no joke. I cannot deal with the absolute chaos of this.

I rinsed Marvin. Partly rinsing myself. And Kareena GD Patel is now acting like my personal saviour here, trying to give me a lifeline for my comedy career.

How much is it? Is this how I make my millions, put myself through law school?

LOL, nah, listen, there is no appearance fee. The show budget is all spent on M&Ms for me. It'll be great for your exposure. Trust me. What's your email? I'll get my people to be in touch with your people. And you can have all the M&Ms you want.

My people is me . . . My email is . . . [redacted].

Listen, I don't know how to tell you that your girl booked her first television appearance off her viral video. It becomes a weird blur of admin before I get to even work out how I feel about it or acknowledge the Kareena-ness of it all, or just be in my feelings for a bit. I just trust in her and it and say yes to everything. I don't even really ask what I'm going to be doing. All I know is, in three days' time, I need to have an excuse ready for my parents as to why I need to go to London. And why I'll be rolling in at 2 a.m. on the last train.

And why I'll probably need the next day off college to really freak the hell out. I haven't even thought about the bit where it gets put on the actual telly. I mean, they won't see it, they never do engage with that sort of stuff. But you never know who might crawl out of the weirdo woodwork and say, 'Hey, uncle, I saw your baby girl on television making jokes with that Gujarati comedian who talks about her periods and how men are the worst. Why isn't she married?'

Evil uncles. Always evil uncles. They hate us and they engage with everything we do in a silent, stalkery way so they can tell on us. They spend more time watching us than watching their own kids, who are running circles all around them. Presumably, they imagine the corresponding uncle will catch their own kids out. The uncle network is vast and creepy as hell.

The producer suggests some trains for me and says they'll send me the tickets. They tell me where to be and what to prepare. They say I'll need to perform five minutes and then do an interview.

And then it hits me.

I need to do five minutes.

Five minutes of material. On television. I've, at this point, had thirty seconds of stage time and that was silence incarnate. I need to practise, surely.

Ding, ding, darling, two weeks till the uni application goes in. Want me to read? My English is terrible of course but I can help. Nagging mum x

A text from Mum breaks the spell of Kareena. Momentarily. Almost irritated with the whole prospect, I write about twenty perfunctory words of the statement, just to make myself feel like I've done something. I pick up a textbook and flick through it like a speed racer before letting it fall in front of me. And then I consider how on earth I can be ready for Kareena's show this weekend.

I can't do this alone, I decide. I am going to need some help. And then, I realise, in classic buddy-cop movie territory, that the only person who can help me is the one I need it from the least. The one who will be the smuggest, most unbearable, absolute idiot-face about it.

I text Leila for the number.

7

'So, young apprentice, let me get this straight,' Jazz says, circling the bench I'm sitting on. We're sitting at the top of St Andrew's Park – it's his local park, which is how I know he's a secret rich boy. It's where he told me to meet him when I said I wanted his help.

'Dude, we haven't got much time. No speeches,' I say.

'Oh, no no no,' he replies. 'Our first lesson. Exactly the type of time I should be making a grand old speech about our intentions. When else do I get to be smug that you need me, you really, really need me?'

'You're going to make this absolutely excruciating, aren't you?' I say, hugging my knees on to the bench as he leans towards me.

'Absolutely I am,' he whispers. 'So, you want to do stand-up, huh? Fine, let's go through the facts. You have been coming to the open mic at LOLZ the last eight weeks, I know this because I was there . . .'

'Doing the same set, week after week,' I mutter.

'Perfecting the same set, week after week,' he declares, throwing his hands out to the world like he is the Jesus of Brazil statue. 'And look, I have been honing my craft. You, my friend, do your first set, bottle it, say not even five words and then boot yourself out the door, declaring your career over. Then your favourite sell-out comedian sees a video of you making fun of some doofus in your college canteen, and now you're on her show, doing stand-up?'

'Why do you care if you think she's a sell-out, Captain Recap?' I ask. 'Sounds like if you asked you to go on her show, you'd tell her to get lost.'

I'm defensive. Kareena is the only role model I've ever had. Not to put too fine a point on it. I don't want to be all, 'I need people to look up to in order to respect myself' and I don't want to be lazy and say, 'She looks like me therefore I should automatically love her', because skinfolk ain't always kinfolk. She's just so funny. And the way she has a freedom to talk about everything, from mental health to her body to the government to the cruelty of white people, to baked goods. She has range, man.

She even does characters. She is so good at setting up a premise at the start of a show or routine and staying within that premise for the entire time. Sure, her show is very mainstream, where she asks guests questions about whatever they're plugging and then sets them up to tell a funny anecdote that shows just how like the rest of us they are, one that has been pre-prepared and signed off. Then they all do some sketches riffing off that week's news. It's worth watching though, because her monologue at the start is always just her.

She has this amazing ability to reel off a script – proper jokes, like it's a thought that just then popped into her head. That ability she has to sound unprepared and unrehearsed, unslick. It's a slickness of its own. I love the way she carries herself too. And also, man, oh man, can someone just be funny?

'That chat show. It's so mainstream. She used to be so cutting edge.'

'You need to have a think about what you're saying. She didn't stop being cutting edge just cos she took a job on a television show. She's still Kareena. But formats is formats. It's a chat show, not a dark Netflix sitcom about addiction and puppetry or something,' I say, spitting literal venom in his direction.

I see him stifle a laugh.

'That TV show, it just ain't for me,' he says.

'Me either,' I admit. 'Her monologues are fire though.'

'Oh,' he stops pacing and sits down next to me. 'I didn't realise she does monologues.' In a lower, embarrassed voice. 'I've never really seen it.'

This makes me crease up. I don't even know if he's being serious but the ridiculous smugness, forced or not, is just so funny to me. I roll into him laughing a loud *ha ha ha ha* type of laugh, hugging my knees, like an egg rolling around perilously.

My dad says I laugh like him. Where every hard consonant of the ha crescendos into the opening of the throat for a coughed ach.

'That's so funny,' I tell him. 'Teach me your ways, brother man.'

'You just need to get up and do it,' he says. He rubs the back of his head.

'Oh, wow, how much do I owe you for this top tip? How to be a better stand-up? Just get up on stage and do it, tell the jokes. Bro, I'm serious. The stakes are high.'

The stakes are really high. Days ago, my dream was over and I was trying to find the most convincing way of lying about wanting to do a law degree on an application form. Literally hours later, I go viral for being funny. Almost like a reminder of why I'm doing this. But these are the stakes you know, ladies and gentlemen. I better tell you some stakes you don't.

Look, it's crushing to run a shop that becomes the pillar of the community and then have a small, branded supermarket open opposite you, in a pure capitalist vulture move, like, 'We see you and we're going to take your business'. And because they sell legit everything, why would you go to them to buy courgettes and luxury chocolate and hipster gin, and then cross the road to Papa and Mum's shop for milk, fags (remember them? LOL), bog roll and the paper. You'd just get it all in one shop. I would. I understand. So would Mum and Papa.

They adjusted and started selling more stuff, but this is now the danger shop. It's so filled with stuff that no one comes in for fresh fruit and veg, which means it's always going off and being binned or turned into experimental soups by Mum.

Meena suggested they find a wholesaler in Birmingham

or London to help sell desi products, like tins of mango pulp and packets of chilli snacks, and all the flavours of the fruit juices.

And they were smashing it. Till the supermarket introduced its world food section.

These people, these companies, are cockroaches. So the shop is open, and empty and it's cheaper to keep it running at a minimal level than it is to get rid of it and incur all the debt that's being kicked into the long grass on it.

Mum and Papa, and their one employee, Sanjana, an exchange student who needs a Saturday job, work long shifts for large portions of the week.

I want them to retire. Mum has this dream of moving to a place with a garden. And tending to the garden. Growing vegetables, getting annoyed about aphids, having streaks of raspberry plants, a patch of food to cultivate and call her own.

I don't think Papa has ever considered retiring. He works too much. I imagine he'd keel over from body shock if he stopped working. But I'm willing to take that chance, you know. Buy him a stack of crime paperbacks and some sudoku books. Force him to golf. Handcuff him to a putter and a nine iron. Make him walk those manicured fields that only let the non-whites play in my preciously short lifetime.

They know I know about the bills and the credit cards that they use to buy stuff from the wholesalers. They even let me pay for the internet and streaming services we all use through my pizza money, because that's how shit it all is.

The law degree is a means to an ends . . . a means to a bigger ends. The end is not the end. You know what I'm trying to say. I want the reign of the shop to end. I hate to be all like, my parents need money, cos that's our business, my friends. Not yours. But hopefully you can relate, because we all do things in life, make choices, all the rest of it, not because of how it affects us, but because of how it could benefit others.

As long as what I do stand-up-wise doesn't affect the plan: rehouse the parents, give mumsy the garden, give papa jaan a golfing stick, then let's do this, Jaswinder.

I run through some jokes with Jazz, some routines, and he's a hard laugher. He reminds me of Meena in that way. He also does not laugh when something amuses him. He tells me it's funny. I think that's because he's analysing everything I'm saying rather than being in the moment and reacting naturally. Also, he's not silly, so I don't sell the silliness of some of my premises in the way that I should.

Where I know I need to inflect or do the act out, I don't. I just sit there, still, and reel off jokes, one by one, to a guy I barely know, who is recording everything in his notebook.

'This is the strangest interrogation ever,' I say at one point. 'It's not even a regulation interview room. Where's the two-way glass?'

'Ma'am, I'm going to need you to focus,' Jazz says, adopting a New Yoik hard-boiled detective growl. 'Where were you on the eighteenth?'

I throw myself on the ground, arms wailing towards the sky.

'Detective, lock me away!' I shout. 'Throw away the key. Put chewing gum in the keyhole. I did it, I tells you. I did it. And I'd do it again if I had the chance. That man did me wrong. Why? No one would believe me, but he deserved it.'

We fall about laughing. I have bypassed his brain.

We spend the rest of the afternoon walking around, refining and rewriting and redefining the jokes. I get more comfortable acting out certain bits. I use my staff discount to get us both cold homemade lemonades from the pizza place. He tests a few of his jokes on me.

I get home in time to reheat food from the freezer for Mum and Papa to eat. When they get back they're both tired.

Papa sits at the kitchen table and removes his socks, folding them before throwing them towards a pile of dirty clothes in front of the washing machine I haven't got to yet. Mum is heating some chillies on the stove.

'You seem different,' she says.

'Happy. Why are you so happy?' Papa demands.

I do feel markedly different for having spent the day talking about comedy with someone, both of us with an implied contract to make each other laugh. It has lifted my spirits for sure. To be doing something I love.

'Is it a boy?' Mum asks.

'What's his name and where do I find him?' Papa adds, miming a backhanded slap to the thigh.

'Oh, he's just a friend,' I say, pulling out clean washing from the machine and creating a new pile, in the doorway, demanding to be hung up around the bathroom.

'Your father was just a friend too,' Mum says, putting the bowl of charred chillies on the table.

'A very good friend,' Papa adds.

'No, he's not a friend like that,' I say, quickly, quickly. 'Not an I-fancy-you-so-I'll-be-nice-to-you friend. He's literally a friend. We both love Kareena Patel and we've just spent the day walking around, hanging out, doing routines. It's been fun. I had fun.'

'Oh,' Papa says. 'He's just a friend.'

This makes Mum laugh and I try not to stomp off with the wet clothes.

8

Jazz meets me at the bus stop and leads me towards Queen's Square. We're heading towards the station where there's a cafe run by a lovely couple of colour, who encourage other non-whites and people from the Queer community to come and hang out. They have poetry stuff some nights, comedy stuff other nights. On Monday nights they show short films by Black Queer creatives. Thursday night is Bollywood night.

Tonight is comedy night. And Jazz wants me to do my stuff in front of a receptive audience that wants me to succeed.

I remind him that skinfolk ain't kinfolk.

'I get you,' he says. 'But this space is for those of us in the margins just to exist. It's about solidarity more than it is about critique. We build our confidence here and we just get to be ourselves here.'

'Look at you, Mr Progressive Future Tory,' I say. 'Why aren't you wearing your usual uniform?'

He's wearing a kurta, which I find hilarious. Like he has different stand-up uniforms for different situations. If he was doing a Saturday night club set amongst the drunks, he might wear a T-shirt with a slogan about how much he holds the woke in contempt, but you know, pithy. Here, with us ethnics, he's ethnicking. A curiosity.

I'm in my standard uniform of black T-shirt, black jeans, white plimsolls. A look that'll never age, and is cheap to maintain, and holds no expectation when my brain has too much in it to budget for decent clothes on top. And it's Kareena Patel's uniform.

I love the vibe of this room. The host is Adibah, someone I used to see around college. With her big David Byrne shoulder pads and short hair, long luminously green nails and snarl, she looks like the coolest dude in the world. There's a bunch more really alluring-looking Black and brown people, all chatting to each other, making it look like the easiest thing in the world to pull off dungarees and boiler suits and slogan T-shirts and crop tops and hoodies all year round, even though the hot swelter of the night is hanging low in this room.

'So, you can do this.' Jazz leans in close to me. 'We rehearsed. At the very least, you know the words you need to say. At best, you say them like you're doing comedy. Whatever happens, stick to the script.'

I've tried it Jazz's way tonight. It's a hard thing to admit that I got stage fright. I didn't even admit it to myself really. So I recorded a set, performed to him, in his car. I had my phone on the dashboard. I looked out on to the street. He sat in the back seat and listened and laughed as needed. And I said my words.

I listened to the recording over and over again, walking

round college, at the back of the library, even in the quieter moments of a few shifts.

I know the script.

'You going up tonight?' I ask, and Jazz nods, of course. He's so focused, he never misses stage time.

I can't quite work out whether he is projecting what he wants on to me and I'm just going with it because Kareena has offered me a lifeline. He told me that he just wants to be on tour, all the time, just doing stand-up.

I ask him who his favourite stand-ups are, and he reels off the sort of list you'd expect from a very serious-about-comedy teenage boy. It's a very studied aggregation of the best stand-up lists. He cites no women, obviously. And only one non-white person, which is super interesting, because he says that person's name specifically in reference to all their early stuff and not all the bad anti-trans stuff they took on as they got more seasoned.

Jazz walks away to talk to Adibah and I watch him. He's being kind to me but I know it's because, whether he'll admit it or not, this Kareena opportunity for me is exactly the type of thing he would love for himself and I'm just living out his dreams for him. Maybe he is hoping that whatever ride I go on, I will take him with me. That's kinda why I invited him. It's a way to say thank you. But also, it's a really weird thing to do all by yourself, so I may as well take someone with me who understands the gravity of the whole thing, even with the ol' sellout rubbish he's peddling.

Jazz is pointing to me and speaking to Adibah, who is smiling like she gets what he's saying. She offers me finger guns and I pretend to fall over, shot by her immaculate aim. You don't miss with nails that deadly. Jazz bounds over to me like a football fan who just got the beers in, elbows out, a wah-hey tremble in his voice and he goes, 'It's sorted.'

Great, great, great. I've been so on autopilot since Kareena's DM that I haven't considered what comes next.

To be the stand-up, you got to do the stand up.

Adibah strides up to the mic and belts out a song line. Everyone except me seems to know it because they belt the next line back to her. She holds the silence for everyone to applaud. She holds a hand to her ear and cranes it towards us all, urging us to show some respect for the night, to warm the space.

'OK, everyone, you know what night it is. It's Safe at Hidden Corner cafe, shouts to Sophia and to Aaron for hosting us as ever. It's a space for us to tell each other our stories. We have poets, comics, musicians all coming up tonight before I take us out with some bass music. This is our space. No one else's. Don't tell the feds, but no whites allowed, right?'

We laugh heartily, safely, knowing that this is a receptive room. I've never been here before. The only way to know about it is through a locked Instagram account that heavily vets who has access. It also has a strict 'if your name's not down, you're not coming in' door policy. The feeling is, well, when you're marginalised – and you may have reasons for keeping yourself, your community, your true self discreet; whether it's community pressure, societal pressure or just you not being ready to do what you need just yet – this is the perfect place to come and engage with art made for you.

Adibah introduces how the evening's going to run and the rules: no lazy 'white people are like so' jokes, no poems about autumnal leaves, no kicking down or sideways on individuals, communities or marginalisations. And, Adibah tells us, if someone has feedback on why your work has negatively affected them, you listen non-judgementally. We all have blind spots. All of us. Even using the words 'blind spot'; I need to ensure that it's not an offensive term. Language is that ingrained in keeping us down. All we can do is hear people and reflect. It's always what we do next that counts.

'First up,' Adibah says. 'Is Madhu Krishna. She doesn't know she's going up but Jazz, her mentor and teacher who taught her everything she knows, said she needs to be jolted into performing. And if she gets in her head too much you won't hear her incredible, hilarious words. So, warm the room, raise the roof, cement the space for . . . Madhu Krishna!'

I elbow Jazz, harder than I mean to but not as hard as I want to. People are applauding and I'm stuck. I can't move. There it is again, the stage fright. The utter, stilting stage fright. The moment where the spotlight is on you and the hum of the microphone is louder than a bomb, and you just cannot move.

People turn to me, because Adibah is pointing, and they all stand up and applaud me. And something weird happens. They all part so there is a gangway down the middle. And those who can, link hands so there's an arch for me to walk down.

I'm drawn to the arch. I slowly inch forward until I'm within it and I'm heading towards the spotlight. Adibah is standing at the end, her hands outstretched towards me.

'You got this.' People whisper encouragement to me as I move painfully slowly through the arch.

'Can't wait for you to share your truth.'

'Go for it.'

'Yes, we're so excited.'

'You're going to do great.'

I finally understand what it is to be held. To be seen. To be accepted. To be me. And that be enough for people. I walk the arch, spudding fists as I go, and my defences soften, so that by the time I reach Adibah and she clutches my fingers and pulls me forward, gently, I feel alive and special and amazing and unbeatable. I practically run up to the microphone.

Jazz put me first for a reason.

No expectation. No time to get in my head. Just time to get up and do it.

I grab the mic and pull it off the stand. It falls to the floor. And I laugh as I bend to pick it up. I do an imaginary curtsy as people whoop and applaud, returning to their seats. I watch Jazz. At the back, arms folded. I have to make him laugh.

'Smooth as ice,' I say into the mic. 'Smooth . . . as . . . ice . . . You'd never be able to tell this was my first time, right?' More whoops, more cheers. 'So yes, my name is Madhu and this is my first stand-up show. You may have seen me . . . go viral for making fun of my mate's ex. Now, you get to suffer through the prepaid stuff. But . . . hecklers beware. Let's go . . .'

I look out at the crowd. It's my crowd. These are my people in front of me. And I understand why Jazz has brought me here.

I beam my way through my set. I talk about everything I need to. I don't even fall back on the script. It all just flows out of me naturally. As if this is the easiest thing in the world to do.

I smile and I soak in the laughs. People are laughing. Well of course they are, I'm awesome. I'm a monster, I'm a monster. The tussle between my entitlement to the microphone and my imposter syndrome is a minimal drone for the five minutes I am up there. I tell jokes about my family, about Mum, about Papa. I steer clear of Meena and her pregnancy and their disowning of her and all that horrible business because that's not for the stage. That's just for me.

I talk about the problems with society (that we all suck), with people's bad pizza takes (that pineapple is fine on pizza), college inconsistencies around dress (that free speech of all kinds is allowed on T-shirt activism in my college, and they consider hate speech free speech). This last bit gathers gasps, and I let those gasps linger before I zing everyone with the final punchline, thank everyone and get the hell off stage to applause and whoops.

And just like that, I've done it. I've done the thing. The thing I knew was possible. I said the words. I got them out. I didn't just get them out. I said them like they belonged to me. I said them like they had meaning and depth and also, they were funny. I was funny. Yes, yes, yes, allow me this, allow me this moment. Let me tell you, I was funny once. That's what matters.

Jazz goes up a few slots later and I watch him, but I'm busy running through every single moment in my set. Basking and buzzing in the moment of my triumph.

In the break, I stand and watch Jazz and Adibah chat. They're celebrating how well I did and it becomes almost weird to have compliments so I smile politely and go to the bar to find a nice herbal tea; something that'll help me climb down from ego mountain.

I'm waiting and a person nods at me. They're wearing a big white T-shirt as a dress and their hair is in a ballet bundle on top of their head. They smile at me.

'That was great,' they say.

'Thank you,' I reply. 'Wild, I can't believe I got to go up.'

'You did, you really did. Listen, I'm about to say this with love because I know you're probably flying from that set, and so you should be. You should be so proud you got up and spoke . . .'

'I feel like there's a but coming . . .'

'Not a but. And I'm not trying to frame this like critique,' they say. 'Wait, hold up, there I am going in and I haven't said hi, properly. I'm Bella. I'm a writer. New to the city. Look, all I wanted to say was, I could listen to you talk about family things all night. I don't want to dictate what you can and can't, will and won't talk about. And the rest of the set was jokes.

But that stuff, it was great. And if you weren't holding back, I think it'd be exceptional.'

I take all this in and smile. I don't know how to reply. I stutter a response. I think they can tell I'm shook. I think I am shook. They're right. I don't want to talk about my family. And yet I do, a little, as a halfway measure. Maybe I should drop it. I mean, it's weird getting feedback in real time like this. I don't like it. I want to live for ever in those first five minutes despite the nature and culture of this night. Even if they're right.

'Yeah, great,' I manage and start to walk away from the bar.

'I'm sorry,' Bella says, calling after me. 'Maybe I was clumsy. I thought that was the nature of the night. Feedback and all. And I'm not saying the other stuff was bad. It was great. I just really settled into your voice when you got personal.'

'Maybe I don't want to get personal,' I say, quite loudly, enough for Jazz to hear my raised voice and scan the room for me.

'I hear you. It's scary. And also, it can be not what you want to use your voice for. Maybe not for now, but it'd be good for you to think about what you want to use your voice for. What stories you might want to tell.'

I nod, stare at my plimsolls, noting new scuffs. I have nothing. In one short interaction, they have deflated me.

I leave the cafe and head for the bus home.

9

On the bus, I spiral.

I argue with Bella in my head. Tell them all the things they need to know. I give them hellfire. I tell them everything about me they need to know in order to make them understand why everything is as it is.

It's so cathartic for a second.

Like, funny's funny. Why does everything have to be personal? A joke is a joke, no? I don't want to put my stuff out there. I just want to make people laugh. No one would dare say what Bella said to a white person.

I open a text to Meena without even thinking about it, but when I realise I've done it I don't know what I want to say. Meena's the one who always encouraged me to try comedy. It was her idea. We just don't flow right now. She left and we stopped communicating properly. Any time we do speak it's functional. How are you and what have you been up to? We skirt around how we really are and what we've really been up to. I want to meet my niece. But I don't dare ask about her. Almost because it would shame me for being silent while Papa waged war on my sister's autonomy and my mum backed him. To ask about my niece, whose name I don't dare speak, would be to admit that I have lost half my family.

I focus back on the undrafted message. Meena would know the right thing to say. She always did. She always told me home truths with actionable ways forward. This is how you are and this is how you can move on. She held me so tenderly in those moments.

I send Kareena a DM.

I'm so nervous about tomorrow.

She replies eerily quickly.

Why? You'll be great. Just be you. That's all we need. You!

How do I know who I am?

Ha! Bit existential for a Thursday night. Look, you know your voice, you know what you want to say. Say that. Again and again until you say it with gusto.

I don't know if I do know my voice. Tonight, I did a set and afterwards someone was telling me what could have been better.

What did they say?

For me to be more personal.

Ahhh, white people. They always want to hear of our pain so they can tick a diversity box. Forget 'em.

I don't correct her. I like what she's saying. Do what I'm doing.

She then adds: **Your comedy got you on my show. Do that.**

Her words panic me. My comedy didn't get me on her show. A video of me making fun of Marvin did.

She goes on: **Just be yourself. Your voice came through in that clip. Your voice is there. Don't you worry at all. I am your new big sister now. We need to stick together. Brown Girls Unite! See you tomorrow.**

Her words cheer me. She is right. My voice is what got me through the set tonight. It's the thing that everyone celebrated. What I had to say and what my view on the world was. Thank god. Because my looks and charm are just what they are, OK?

Kareena Patel, my new big sister.

I thank Kareena for the 'coach in the locker room, one foot up on the bench, before the big game' pep talk and she sends me back a thumb emoji, which usually signals the end of any conversation. By this point, I've reached home.

As I walk through the flat, I hear the soft murmur of machine-gun fire from an action film Papa will be watching in the dark with subtitles on. That must mean Mum is asleep. I go to my room and take my socks off and flex my toes in the fresh air. I ease myself on to the bed and stare at the picture of Kareena and recite my script again, just to be sure it's in my head.

Tomorrow is another day. Also, tomorrow is *the* day.

10

Jazz meets me at Temple Meads with a brown paper bag and a coffee.

'I bought you a croissant,' he says after I gratefully take the cup. 'You didn't text me back. I was worried you were dead.'

I fell asleep reciting my lines cos I was so tired, and he messaged me a bunch of times with code words to use if I was in trouble or dead.

This morning, I figured I was seeing him in a few hours so didn't need to send a message as well. The power of surprise and all that.

'Jaswinder, Madhu has been dead for ten years,' I say, spookily, floating my body all around him, into oncoming commuters who tut like they've never accidentally got in anyone's way before.

'She won't want this almond croissant in that case,' Jazz says, dangling the bag. I grab it snarling, like, gimme. 'Only problem is, it's vegan . . .'

'Dammit,' I say, my face crumbling. 'The butter's the best bit!'

'I know . . . well, I don't know, I'm vegan,' Jazz says.

'Yes, you mention it three times in your set, and I'm not

counting the bit where you reference how often vegans tell us they're vegan.'

I wait till we're on the train, sitting across from each other at a table that has not been cleaned of the dust from older pastries than mine and smears of commuter-go-juice. The taping's at 6 p.m. with enough time for it to be edited for airing at 11 p.m., and we're to arrive at the studio at 4 p.m., but we're getting to London for 11 a.m. because I've never been and Jazz wants to go and have lunch at a cafe where three of his favourite comedians dreamt up his favourite comedy character. He wants to sit at their table and tell a joke.

I need his support so I'm happy to indulge him. Especially as it's not far from where Kareena's show films.

I woke up with Kareena's final message in my mind. *Just be yourself.* My self is what got us on to the show in the first place. Maybe my voice is just me. That's OK, right? To be unfiltered me.

That thought carried me through as I got ready. Standard Madhu uniform in operation – though significantly, not just any black T-shirt this time but the one that I don't wear too often because it's the type of material that fades and I get to roll the slightly baggy sleeves up like I'm a badass. Same with the jeans – they've faded just the right amount to seem like I've toured hard in them, worn them to every comedy club, sweated out the hot nights; they stink of grime and mic juice and the unwashed seat covers of green rooms up and down the land.

They're my lucky jeans. I only wear them on dates and gigs.

And both of those were science fiction till about a week ago. So now they're my gig jeans. Who has time to date when you're about to appear on your comedy-hero big sister's late night chat show?

Jazz asks to reread the producer's briefing notes to get a sense of what I'm doing. He likes to prepare. I like to just feel out what I'm doing. He opens a notebook and pushes my phone back to me across the table.

'Tell me . . . tell me what you're going to talk about.'

'What do you mean? Just gonna answer the questions. They'll ask a question and I'll answer it.'

'This first one. Imagine I'm Kareena. "So, tell me about going viral. What's that like?"'

I shrug. I don't know how to answer him, if I'm being honest. I haven't really taken much notice of it. I signed up for a Twitter account, was found by Kareena and that's been the sum of my world. A whole day later and everyone had moved on to something else. A new version of a meme. Another way to do a 'how it started, how it's going', but for TV show characters. And that was that. I didn't feel deflated. I didn't feel relieved. I didn't feel elated that I'd had my five minutes of fame. I just came and went and I got, perfectly, what I wanted. Someone memed me saying 'what's wrong with men?' and I saw that being used. But mostly, I don't really log in to Twitter. It's just there on my phone. As unused as my fitness apps and other things you download on a whim thinking it will help form a brand new habit which will change your life. When actually, all I need is WhatsApp and Candy Crush.

'It was all right,' I say, and I shrug again.

Jazz erupts, leaning all the way across the table.

'This is your moment,' he says, almost like he's my boxing coach and I'm one round out from winning the title. 'You have been given this shot. You can't throw it away. This is a game. Everybody plays. She asks you questions because you're this week's viral celebrity, and she likes that you're brown, yay diversity, tick a box. That's her game. Yours is, how do I turn this into a career so when I go to uni, I'm doing the lectures yawning and I'm turning in the essays a day late, and I am hitting the clubs, in London, or Manchester, or Birmingham every night, going up once, twice, maybe, just to prove I can do it.'

'Prove to who, coach?' I ask, and this shuts Jazz up.

We have a couple of minutes of awkward silence where I stare at my blank phone screen as distraction.

'I've read the questions,' I say. He doesn't look up; he's writing in his notebook. 'I've formulated some idea of what I'll say. I chatted to Kareena last night. She was like, just be you. Nothing to worry about. I'm just going to be me.'

I want to show Jazz my late-night exchange with Kareena, but in this moment, it feels private. And then I'm interrupted by the buffet trolley.

'Get you anything, love?' the person says to the man across the aisle from me.

I wait patiently for my moment. The man orders a tea and a

porridge and both are prepared like there isn't the rest of the entire train to service. Which the man loves. Obviously his card is declined and he demands it be retried until it does and then he gives up and pays in cash.

The buffet trolley person moves past us and I clear my throat as loudly and obnoxiously as I can. They turn back to me and look to see if I'm OK.

'Good sir,' I say in my most Jane Austeny voice, my dourest, poshest, Thomas Hardyest voice. 'I do believe you will find that you skipped my good man and my good self.'

Jazz looks up. He is invested in the bit.

'Oh,' the buffet trolley person says. I know what they're thinking. *These teens don't have any money. What could they possibly want? We don't sell in-app purchases or Haribo.* 'Sorry, what can I get you?'

'My good friend and I, good sir, will have the best thing on the menu. Or the most expensive. Whichever costs more.'

'I believe the most expensive thing will cost the most,' the buffet trolley person says, confused.

'Is it also the best?'

'Look, we have a lovely Côtes du Rhône. Bottled three years ago. Very fruity, very light, a table wine . . .'

'Good sir,' Jazz says, joining in on the bit. 'My good friend and my good self are underage. You couldn't possibly entertain servicing our good selves with good alcohol, could you?'

'Please may I see some ID?' the buffet trolley person says.

It takes everything within me to not burst into laughter.

'My good sir, my good friend and I have not chosen to partake of any alcohol. What is one's most expensive crisp?'

'Any truffle and caviar flavours?' Jazz asks, and I lose it.

The buffet trolley person leans into me.

'You think you're the only one who can do silly voices?' they hiss. Then they put on a high-pitched squeal of a voice. 'Hello, I am a funny teenager. I think everything I do is original, wah wah wah, please can I have some money?'

I cut eyes with Jazz but he has his fist in his open mouth, his eyes clenched shut like fruit and a throaty algae leaking up and down his vocal chords.

'One will have salt and vinegar,' I say, and you know what, even the buffet car person laughs.

Our arrival in London makes my chest tight. I know Meena is in the city and I'm choosing to not see her. That's really bad of me. I've not even met my niece yet.

We fall into single file with everyone else trying to get out of the station. Jazz wants us to walk to this legendary cafe. He tells me about visiting London a lot over the years and seems to know where everything is. It's a nice day and a short Tube ride so we decide to save our squids and walk.

We walk past an old-looking house with fancy windows. He points up to the top.

'That's Mum's flat,' he says, absent-mindedly. 'I wonder if she's at home.'

Huh?

'She doesn't live in Bristol? With you?'

'Oh yeah, of course. She just works a lot so stays here when she needs. Like three or four days a week.'

'Damn, so mostly just you and your dad, huh?'

'Nah, he's in Dubai ten months of the year. He comes back for the rainy season. The month of November and the month of February.'

'Damn, I'm so sorry. I didn't realise your parents had split.'

Jazz looks at me. 'They haven't split,' he tells me. 'Why did you think that?'

I don't ask him any more because I can see his shoulders tense when he talks about them. It's hard to not make some stereotypical judgements at this point, ladies and gentlemen. He lives in a well posh bit of Bristol, his mum has a central London flat near a big train terminus and his father lives and works in Dubai. He has three homes. I knew there was a reason a seventeen year old might own one of those navy blue 'I'm a serious adult in casual mode' blazer things.

I think Meena lives in South London. That much I have gleaned from what she's told me. I don't know the geography of it, so I couldn't tell you where. But I still expect her to jump out at any second, even though I know the city is huge.

As if he can read my mind, Jazz asks me, 'Hey, is your sister coming?'

I shake my head.

'She's not coming?'

'I didn't invite her,' I say, curtly, loudly, enough for him to get

93

the message, and I begin our crossing of the road.

On the other side of the road, Jazz won't quit.

'That's so weird, right? I know your family is beefing or whatever but it's your big day, no?'

'Why aren't you popping in to see your mum? We literally just walked past her flat.'

Jazz lengthens his body, like a pencil wanting to be chosen in a desk tidy. He points at a familiar coffee chain, and mutters something that I assume is about going in to get some coffee. I wait outside for him.

He emerges with two coffees. He offers one to me but I keep my hands in my jeans pockets, forcing him to double-park two coffee cups as we walk towards this legendary cafe.

So far, my impressions of the capital city are: lots of people, lots of statues of weird colonisers, lots of tourists and lots of cobbled streets where you'd least expect them, a pox on my poor ankles.

Someone has written 'Mad' on my cup. I side-eye Jazz.

'I gave up spelling it about halfway through. We're almost there – the cafe is just round the corner,' Jazz tells me.

'What is it with you and this place, anyway?' I'm irritated because I want to pee, and I'm a little angry that he pushed me about Meena. Even if he might be right. Probably because he is right.

'Are you kidding? It's where everyone used to go for fry-ups after the midnight set at the Comedy Store. All the greats ate here and tried out new material on each other.'

I roll my eyes – Jazz is just so typical of every guy I know. All his heroes are white men, like a female comic doesn't even get a look in. Never mind a brown funny girl.

'Why do you hate Kareena so much?' I confront him.

'I know you want me to admit it's because she's a brown girl and I have all this internalised misogyny against my sisters, but the truth is, it's just not my thing,' he says.

'No, rubbish,' I reply. I bang a passing lamppost for emphasis. 'I want the *truth*,' I demand in a big movie actor way.

'You can't handle it,' he replies. 'Seriously, what kind of guy would I have to be if that's what I thought?'

'I just don't get it . . .'

'If I hated brown girls so much, why am I helping you?' he asks.

'Cos you're patronising me,' I say, laughing, knowing it's not true, but also knowing his panic will lead him closer to my trap.

'Sis, you're having a laugh. I'm helping you cos I think you're well funny,' he says. 'Kareena just doesn't seem real, that's all. When I see her on her show and on panel shows and stuff, I feel like she's acting. Like I couldn't tell you the real her. Because I just don't know who that is.'

'And should that matter? She's in the public eye,' I reply, outraged. 'She's entitled to keep us all at a huge distance, surely?'

Like he is entitled to everything that she isn't public about. Like her life is there for him to consume.

'You're an idiot,' I say. 'She's not our friend. She doesn't

95

deserve the level of scrutiny she gets about how real she is when you cite an invented character comedian as one of your favourites.'

'We're here,' Jazz says, and I look up at this nondescript spot. Specialty Cafe is an odd-looking place, out of step with the rest of the street, with the rest of London, with the rest of the country. It is tiled like a bathroom and the tables and chairs are all plastic garden furniture.

'Oh, look,' I say, pointing at the entirely tiled, wall-to-floor interior of the cafe. 'We have those tiles in our bathroom as well.'

Jazz smiles as he opens the door.

11

The cafe is owned by an old couple who scream at each other the entire time we're there. They have one register for order-taking, order-collecting and general irritation. And that's loud arguing, in a mixture of Italian and English. Their daughter and son, who act as table service, do so in silence. They are under the rule of this couple. He is fat with undone buttons at both ends of his shirt. And she is small and thin with her hair tied back into a tight top bun, pulling her entire face upwards like she is a cartoon character. An oldies station plays out the same songs Papa plays in the shop.

The cafe is empty and looks like it hasn't seen much trade since the breakfast rush. Jazz and I definitely feel the eye of attention from the family. Maybe because we're teenagers. Maybe because we're their only clients. But their attitude is very, why are you here? Why aren't you in school?

We sit in the window like Jazz's favourite comedians and I sip at some tepid tap water while Jazz writes in his notebook. Now we've stopped, I check the time and realise that I'm going on Kareena Patel's show. In a few hours. My god. My actual god.

Like I was just on auto pilot this whole way and even though

Jazz is an idiot who annoys me, I'm glad he has irritated me enough for me to not remember that I'm going on national television with my actual hero today. I've done everything to not think about it.

Jazz looks up from his notebook.

'Here's the thing about tea-drinkers . . .' he says, and I roll my eyes. He stops. 'What?'

'Tea-drinkers? Really? That's your joke?' I ask, Bella's criticisms still coursing through my veins.

'What's in your heart, man?' I ask.

Jazz laughs and carries on writing. 'Don't do that,' he says, to his notebook.

'Do what?'

'Project your own stuff on to me. I mean, I get why that random shook you. But they can't shake me. I know what I'm about.'

I realise I didn't even tell Jazz what they'd said. How did he know? I start gathering my things. I know I'm not going anywhere. I want answers. I feel like this urgency will make him not try and take me for a walk with his reply.

'Hey, sit down. What's going on?'

The waitress brings over our lunches at this exact point. She puts his vegan breakfast in front of him and tries to land my plate but I shake my head and ask her to take it back.

'Can you believe it?' I say to the waitress. 'He's been chatting about me and my issues to strangers. Isn't that so gentlemanly of him. Talking about me behind my back.'

The silent waitress looks back at her parents and then to me, confused.

'She's talking rubbish, ignore her, I'll have it.'

The waitress puts down my half stack with bacon in front of Jazz and he looks at it then me.

'Did you put them up to it?' I ask.

'Put who up to what?' he says, forking his vegan sausage and taking a bite.

I slowly drag my plate across to my side of the table. The maple syrup is very thick, the bacon is very sad-looking; they've used back bacon rashers instead of those hard crispy streaks. There's a polite basil leaf in the middle of the plate - a visual reminder to not neglect your greens, I guess.

'Bella, the person who came up to me after my set and started going off about what was working and what wasn't . . .'

'If you must know,' Jazz says. 'I saw you leave looking annoyed and I didn't want to chase you down the street in case you needed space, so I asked Bella what they'd said to upset you. And they told me they gave you feedback as that's the spirit of the night . . .'

'So? They were rude.'

'I took you there for a reason, Madhu. That's the point of those nights. They hold you so you perform in the best way possible and then they give you honest critique because we don't have to just like each other's stuff because we're brown. We have to push each other to be better. That's what that night's function is. You didn't take it in the way it was intended.'

I stab my half stack and stand the fork upright in it.

'You could have warned me, man,' I say. 'I know you're just trying to help me. But at the same time, you have to remember I'm so delicate about this stuff.'

'It's because you thought you'd be amazing at it before you tried it, isn't it?' he says, staring at his portobello mushroom, trying to work out where to stab it to pick it up whole. He eats everything on his plate, one item at a time. He doesn't vary what's in his mouth or on his fork. He eats the sausage till it's gone then the beans till they're gone then the mushroom till it's gone, and eventually the plate is stripped of any evidence there was once a delicious plant-based breakfast on it.

'What do you mean?' I ask.

'Well,' he says. 'Bella was right. You can dig deeper. We had a battle to get you onstage. One thing at a time.'

'Oh,' I say. 'Jazz knows best, does he?'

'You asked for my help,' he tells me.

'You sent me up to do a set knowing it wasn't my best,' I reply. 'That's mean.'

I retrieve the fork and stab the half stack again, this time twisting the fork to create a well in the middle.

'Sorry,' he mumbles.

'Listen, I don't know where you get off telling me that I'm arrogant or whatever, but I have a reason to do this, I have painful things to work out. I didn't live a semi-charmed life of butlers and actually celebrating Christmas. I didn't come to anything expecting it to be good. I came to it knowing I cannot ever do this as a living. Never. No matter how good I might be, no matter how good I could be with some practice and with some nurturing. That's not the life for me. I have to work, earn money. I have to pay for things. You don't need to worry about anything do you, *rich boy*? You literally have three homes.'

I fork out the middle of the half stack now I've loosened it with a twisting fork and I shove it into my mouth. I grimace at him. He's staring at me, waiting for the moment to say I'm finished. I chew slowly, and hold a finger up to let him know more is coming.

'So thank you for joining me on this adventure. But remember why you're here. You're not helping me to make me better, because we both know this is a holiday for me. I could be the best comic in the world and no one will ever know, because I know what my life has to be. You, on the other hand – this is just part of the networking trail that rich boys like you are accustomed to. So when I introduce you to Kareena, you'll be nice and complimentary and you'll make friends with everyone you can, in the hope that you can grab their contacts and message them about your own stuff. The problem is, buddy, I've seen your material. Repeatedly. The same five jokes about the same five things. They're great observations, but it's hardly your blood on the page, is it?'

Jazz looks down and writes 'blood on the page' in his notebook before drawing a circle around it.

'Is that *blood* on the page? Or blood *on* the page? I just want to get the emphasis right,' he says. 'For the nuance of it, you know?'

'You work it out,' I say, cutting up some bacon and plunging it into the maple syrup congealing around my plate. 'You seem to have all the answers.'

We leave before Jazz gets to tell me a joke, which I feel bad about, it's the one thing he asked for us to do, but the vibes are off, so we don't. I don't tell him I feel bad though. We're about a twenty-minute walk from the studio and we have an hour to spend, which I do by walking into every single shop I can. I look through the shelves of a bookshop, picking out a couple of things that I want to read before discarding them. No money. Jazz offers to buy them and I decline, giving him the tone of voice that says it isn't a question of whether I can afford to buy them or not, monetarily speaking. It's about the hard decisions you make about what to spend that money on. I say all this with my eyes; I'm really cool.

Something about all this time we need to pad out makes me panic when we leave the bookshop, so I sit on the floor and take a deep breath.

'We need to be there in five,' Jazz says.

'I know,' I reply. 'I just need a minute.'

Jazz sits down next to me, an uncomfortable cross-legged position, hand on the floor, leaning back, wishing for a lounge chair to magically appear.

'So my family has money, so what?'

'Wow, you should lead with that at your next homeless charity gala,' I say. 'So, my family has money, so what? One of my three homes could house half of you here . . .'

'Wait, so homeless people are coming to a homeless gala? Aren't those tickets expensive?'

'I don't know, but why would you have a homeless gala without actual homeless people there? Feels weird . . .'

'I mean, it's for rich people to go and donate money to a cause while they eat an expensive meal. It's weird. Like competitive donating, or something. Could have just saved everyone some money and done a direct debit from home . . .'

'Imagine being a billionaire and waking up every day thinking, my espresso machine is too noisy, and not, oooh, maybe I'll fund youth clubs all over the country. Why don't your mum and dad fund youth clubs all over the country?'

'They're massive capitalists and I hate it, yes. And yes, I've benefitted from that life. But I'm trying, innit, I'm trying.'

'By telling jokes?' I ask. I laugh. I laugh some more. I fold my arms in front of me and lean forward, laughing and laughing.

'What's so funny?' Jazz asks, lifting up into a squat, ready to go, thinking my moment has passed.

'The billionaire's son saved the world with jokes. Wow,' I say, looking up at him. 'What a story. What an inspiring story. Who'd play you in the movie biopic? Someone with sweet eyes. Maybe Dev Patel. Who'd play me? Scarlet Johansson.'

'Why are you so angry with me about my family? I didn't ask

to be born,' he replies, standing up and looking at his phone. 'It's half past, by the way . . .'

'I didn't ask to be born?' I repeat with a shrill whine, in an unflattering impression of him. I know as I do it, it's really not cool but I just cannot stop myself. 'No one asks to be born. And no one can help the family they're born into. What they can do is not self-aggrandise about how, despite all this, they're a better person. No one cares if you tell jokes, Jazz. No one. In years to come, joke boy, you'll become an estate agent like the rest of them, and you'll just go about your day, trying to sell idiots small flats with broken showers and being a fascist about references.'

Jazz shakes his head.

'I know why you're picking a fight with me . . .'

'Why?' I bellow, loudly, performing to the street. 'Because I'm nervous. So I'm nervous and picking on you – it doesn't make what I said untrue. It's just that the nerves leaked my private thoughts. So what?'

Suddenly I want to go home. I don't feel right or ready. Those people who feel entitled to perform, to make stuff, to prioritise what they have to say above what everyone else does, they have something special that I just don't. How do they get that? I don't understand it. For as long as I've been in school or college or work, I've seen that there are two types of people in the world. The curious and the expert. The curious person asks questions of the world. The expert knows all the answers. Sometimes, they, like, *actually* know. Other times, they just want you to know they know. I hate those people. Jazz feels like that to me. He projects cool, calm expertise because it means he doesn't have to show me his real face . . . which is probably smeared in truffle oil.

'I want to go home,' I tell Jazz.

'No you don't,' he replies.

'My god, man, have you learned nothing? I want to go home. Doesn't mean I'm going to. This isn't a movie filled with dramatic gestures. I can't just leave now and go home and leave everyone in the lurch.'

Jazz nods and considers this. He turns and walks in the direction of where I assume the television studio is.

'What do you think is the worst that'll happen?'

'That she'll hate me . . .'

'So?'

'My hero will hate me. And that, after she reopens the door to my comedy career, it'll go badly and I'll want to give up; that my dad will watch it and kill me for lying about where I am; that my sister will watch it and kill me for making fun of our family; that the uni admissions people at Bristol will see it and not offer me a place for a law degree; that my boss at the pizza place will see it and confess his undying love for me, because he definitely does love me – why wouldn't you? And that you'll tell me I'm not funny.'

I stop in the street, shoulder-barged by a tutting passer-by.

'What?' I scream at them. 'Never stopped in the street to wrestle with a dark thought?'

They turn to me and stop.

'Sorry, you're right . . .'

'Excuse me?' I say.

'I'm running late for an audition, and *I'm* the reason I'm late. Nerves I guess. They made me spiral. And so I took it out on you by acting like you were the reason I'm late. Sorry about that.'

'It's OK,' I say. 'And hey, thank you for saying sorry. And good luck in the audition.'

This last bit breaks their face. They smile, somewhat hopefully, nodding at me, swivelling on their Chelsea boot and walking in the direction of a part they were born to play.

I breathe in deeply the way Danny taught me as a way of dealing with anxiety on my first night of taking orders. Serving up, remembering things requested in passing, clearing tables, resetting tables – it was overwhelming that first night. I'd never seen a place so busy. Breathe in for a count of four, and breathe out for a count of eight, Danny had shown me. 'Do this four times in total and you'll find your breath regulated to the flow of the room,' I could hear him telling me now.

I breathe in – one, two, three, four.

I breathe out – one, two, three, four, five, six, seven, eight.

I see Kareena in my head, doing stand-up. I'm not watching it on YouTube, I'm in the room, my skin is hot from the airless basement, my mind is racing with ideas, she is speaking, and I cannot hear a word, but I am beaming.

I breathe in – one, two, three, four.

I breathe out – one, two, three, four, five, six, seven, eight.

She brings me onstage and I stand up from the front row of the crowd, spinning around, arms windmilling, legs jigging, and I bow to my crowd. They're all faceless as they applaud.

I breathe in – one, two, three, four.

I breathe out – one, two, three, four, five, six, seven, eight.

I edge backwards towards the stage, my arms outstretched. Kareena reaches under my arms and hoists me up. I stand up. I grab the microphone, I grin.

I breathe in – one, two, three, four.

I breathe out – one, two, three, four, five, six, seven, eight.

I open my eyes and nod to Jazz, a determined 'let's go'. He leads the way to the television studio.

12

The security guard doesn't let us into the building. He thinks we're teenage star-stalkers. He tells us to go away, despite me pleading that I'm on the show tonight. When I say the name of the producer, Hannah, he laughs at me.

'Anyone can say Hannah. This industry is run by Hannahs. How do I know you mean a Hannah that works here and you're not just saying Hannah because that's a very likely name?'

Jazz huffs and puffs, hands on his hips. Finally, he understands what it's like to have your access into a space denied.

'Uncle,' I say, playing the brown people in white spaces solidarity card. 'Kareena has booked me on her show. Like, why else would I be here? All I'm asking is to check in at reception. If my Hannah ain't your Hannah, they'll call you and tell you to get me to leave. Why are you embarrassing us in front of the whites, uncle? They already don't trust any of us.'

The security guard looks into the glass windows of the glamorous television studio by the water and looks back at me.

'You promise you won't stalk anyone?'

'Who would I stalk?' I ask.

'gridlock's performing tonight.'

'gridlock?' Jazz says. 'I love his work.'

'Exactly,' the security guard says. 'Exactly.'

'Please, uncle, I'm already late.'

'Go on, then. But if you are thrown out, I will use my taser. I just upgraded to a new one and I haven't had the opportunity to try it out yet.'

'That is . . . wild,' Jazz says as I push my way through a heavy glass door.

The reception for the television studio is very white – both people-wise and décor-wise. Lots of sharp edges on the furniture, to match the cool edge of the shows they think they're making, probably. Lots of big vases of water with whole lemons at the bottom. A perfectly fanned crescent of magazines that look untouched.

Two busy receptionists, headsets in, talking, talking, talking.

People walking through, drinking coffee out of competitive reusable cups. A person sits by herself, in a red skirt and open-toe sandals. She looks our age. With the off-white shirt too, she definitely is wearing the uniform of the first day of work experience. I say this because I wore the same thing the first day of my week's work experience with a construction law firm back home.

The receptionist at the desk looks up at us and smiles – so fake. Jazz stiffens, going into business mode, like he's my manager. I guess he has to feel useful. Before he can speak, I step in front of him.

'Hi,' I say.

'Are you here for the diversity day? It doesn't start for another two . . .'

The receptionist is tapped on the shoulder by her colleague, who leans over.

'Sis,' she says. 'The way you rinsed that little boy was hilarious. Me and my people have been watching that video again and again all week. You here to do Kareena's show, yes?'

I nod, instantly befuddled by my fame. Like it doesn't really exist. Like it belongs to someone else. Like I haven't earned it. I put my elbows on their desk and lean forward, my head dipping as low as I can get it, breathing again, my chest shallow.

The room is edging in on me. I can't speak, suddenly. Like a dry throat. Like a flutter in my stomach. Like a tongue that lies flat. Why am I trying to compare it to some random relatable thing for you when I can just let you know I forget how to talk. Like someone who has been hypnotised to feel like their mouth is glued shut.

'Yes she is,' Jazz steps forward, thinking he's rescuing me and I shuffle to block him. He's not my manager.

'Yep,' I say, tipping down some imaginary sunglasses, playing the part of the 'talent', which is what the TV producer kept calling me in all the emails. 'I am here to do Kareena's show, yes.'

'Great. Cool beans,' the receptionist says. 'I'll get Hannah

110

to come down and fetch you. They'll take you to where you need to go.'

She points to a sofa that has no back. It's white and leather and squelches as I sit on it. I'm starting to find Jazz's presence an annoyance. I feel overstimulated by having to modulate myself in front of him instead of disappearing into a comedy album on my phone. He sits next to me and asks whose is the most famous bottom that has ever sat on this sofa. I don't answer him. I'm taken with a poster of Kareena on a wall of other framed luminaries to the right of the reception desk. She is beaming as she clutches her side with one hand and her clutching hand with her other hand. Like she's got a handle and a seatbelt on. She's wearing a black T-shirt and black jeans. And she looks so happy. I don't know when this photo was taken. Maybe it was when she had her big break. Maybe she was told, 'Smile, it might never happen' or something else patronising. Maybe she was just in the mode to feel like it was all happening.

I try to imagine what was going through her head when that photo was taken.

Kareena got famous when she was in her final year of her degree. She started posting these videos that went viral really quickly, of her as a coach for white guys trying to date brown girls. They were so funny and acerbic. Like, one of them was all about the minefield of acceptable questions on a date and what was a microaggression and what wasn't. It wasn't just casual racism bingo. It was also related to something in the news. She took the government to task by observing their racism and turning it into what it must be like to go on dates with these hateful idiots.

She finished up her degree with a 2:2 and celebrated by going to Edinburgh for the first time on the Free Fringe. Legend has it that her show, which she released on her SoundCloud that autumn, is all true. She had gone up to Edinburgh to do stand-up for a summer before doing the whole sensible job thing with a graduate scheme. Kareena just wanted to tell jokes. She just wanted to make people laugh. She loved the feeling – as she described in a podcast interview about comedy techniques – of bypassing people's brains with jokes and making them laugh at things that ultimately made them feel uncomfortable.

Her girlfriend, who was in a play that year on the Free Fringe, had got Kareena a slot doing fifteen minutes of a line-up of four comedians, also on the Free Fringe. She'd go on, then another person, then another, then another. They could vary the order if they wanted. She got dumped on the first night and none of the other comedians showed up for their slots. Two couldn't get enough money together to come up, another got upgraded to the proper Fringe cos her show was so popular and Kareena suddenly had to fill an hour. And given she had nowhere else to stay but in the house-share she and her girlfriend were planning to be a part of, and her girlfriend was now together with another of her cast mates, well, Kareena slept in the cast mate's bed and went to sleep listening to the sounds of her ex-girlfriend having a lovely old time with someone else through the thin, cheap walls.

And thus her first hour was born. An ongoing documentation of the horror of her life.

The audience grew, compelled by the different set every night, growing in truth and depth as Kareena made them all laugh, talking about heartbreak and disaffection and isolation, about being the only brown girl in the middle-class white household of her nightmares, about Edinburgh being an unforgiving space for a minority and about how this was meant to be her dream.

It was hilarious.

I only heard the recording she did towards the end of the run when the world had been built and the hour was sorted. But it was so legendary, it got uploaded to SoundCloud and then turned into a Radio 4 show and then a memoir and then a sitcom pilot in a season of other sitcom pilots by diverse talents that never got made into something longer because ultimately it was a box-ticking exercise and not a shot at the big time. Or so she said in an interview months after it aired. All the while, she was touring and developing the show, and touring some more and she left the graduate scheme after a year of, amazingly, turning up to work every day and gigging two or three nights a week, and a nationwide tour where she always got to where she needed to and then back in time for work. Her discipline and motivation were amazing. Then she finished the graduate scheme and did her next Edinburgh show, all about the graduate scheme. And then more tours, two more shows, and then her chat show. She was now certified legend status.

I don't want to be one of those 'never had anyone who looked like me' bores who ignore all the people in right-wing governments who look just like them, but it was powerful. Maybe it was the doing the degree and being a spiky brown girl. Maybe it was the similar background. Maybe it was just the colour of our skin being similar.

I followed her everywhere I could. And I devoured everything I could. She was so funny, man, what can I tell you? And then she told a politician who had got embroiled in a racism scandal (the scandal: no one except brown and Black people was willing to admit publicly that she was a racist) that they were a liar and a racist on a news panel show, and then the press came for her. That's when they found her bikini shots on a private Facebook, literally on a family holiday, and they found the one white guy she had dated to talk about her, and they found videos of her making fun of white people and said she was the real racist. Before you could say, wow, the country really hates people calling out racism more than it hates racism, her chat show got pulled off the air. And then, she got the last laugh because a big streaming site bought that chat show, gave it more money and gave her access to premium Hollywood stars, to big musical guests, and to a catalogue of swear words. It was glorious. This is the point where Jazz thinks she sold out. And it's the point at which I think she became certified gangster.

I watch the stairs nervously, thinking Kareena is about to emerge – about to run down and say hi and give me the hug I've always needed. I'm not saying I'm hug-deficient. Just, you know, a good one from a stranger who you are a bit in love with is pretty cool.

Jazz is writing in his notebook.

I stick in my earphones and listen back to one of Kareena's comedy albums on my phone and close my eyes. I have that agitated sleep jerk – the one where you start to drift off but noises, and nerves, keep pulling you back into the room. It makes me more tired than I am ... I don't even want the sleep ... I just need to not stare at the stairs ... Like they're an ascension to the pantheon of the comedy gods ... Like they're—

I hear my name and I open my eyes. I must have drifted off for like, a minute, which is worse than ten minutes, which is worse than twenty minutes.

I open my eyes, to see her – to see Kareena – crouching down to me, sunglasses perched on her head, tiny Matrix-like things, coffee cup, gold and clutched near my face. The aroma of the beans is like smelling salts.

Oh god, I am listening to her while she's waking me up.

I sit, bumping the coffee cup and wrenching the earbuds out, letting them drop to my lap.

'Hey,' Kareena Patel says. 'Hey there. Madhu Krishna, the gangster herself, what's up, what's up?'

I stare at her a bit too long. Her skin shimmers, she smells like shea butter and her hair falls in line perfectly behind her ears. She's wearing a black rollneck and black jeans. She has a black backpack on and she is squinting.

'Are you listening to me?'

I nod, cringing with my entire body, trying to wrench the earbud wire out of my phone as quickly as I can.

'I mean, that's pretty awkward, no?' I nod again. 'Listen, Madhu, we'll meet properly later. I have to go and shout at the writers till they make me sound funny so I'll see you in a bit. In the meantime, don't listen to my old stuff. There's much better than me ten years ago out there, innit.' She pauses. 'Like my special from last year. That's iconic, no?'

I smile as she spins around and disappears into the maelstrom of people who seem to be waiting for her. A mixture of producers? Agents? Managers? Assistants? It's like a phalanx of important people to protect the super important person from anyone unimportant. They all smile at me like in this moment I am important. I watch my hero disappear into the offices and look at my phone, wanting to throw it across the room for snitching on me.

'That was excruciating,' Jazz says, and I have no option but to burst out laughing in agreement.

13

We're moved from one sofa to another, this one closer to the studio. Apparently there are no dressing rooms free for me because one of the actors who is a guest tonight has demanded two: one for them and one for their masseuse.

Who knew living the dream would involve so much sitting?

Who knew living the dream would involve witnessing people panic because a teenager doesn't have a dressing room?

Jazz even leans over to me at one point and says, 'It's wild how the dressing room is what's upended things and not the fact that you're unaccompanied . . .'

'You're here,' I say.

'Neither of us are over eighteen. You need a parent or guardian.'

I laugh, thinking, *Wow, yes, a child protection nightmare is about to happen.*

'If it goes badly, I'll sell this story to the papers and make my millions,' I tell him.

'Or even better, tell them now and watch how they freak out even more.'

The fact that the scrabbling people are doing their best to

make me feel comfortable, even though I'm the lowest of the lowest bit of the pecking order, is amusing me. Because why should I get anything? A dressing room? Snacks? Or anything at all? I'm literally just a kid who went viral and is currently missing a Spanish exam to be here.

Señora Flint is going to be so annoyed.

Jazz asks if I want a cup of tea and disappears in search of a kettle and some teabags while I sit and wait. Everyone who walks past seems so busy, everything they're doing so urgent, so important. Each of them pauses to take me in and try to remember who on earth I am and why on earth I am sitting here like a lemon getting dryer by the second.

Papa calls and I let it ring to voicemail. Mum calls and I let it ring to voicemail. I text Meena and ask her how she is. I see the bubbles of her considering her reply before it goes to unanswered.

Papa has left a voicemail asking me to get a few vegetables from the shop on the way home. Some bhindi and some karela. Two of my least favourite things but he does crave them at least once a month. The sheer mundanity of his request, coupled with the lie I've told to come and experience the true mundanity of my dream job, makes me well up. All the nerves crash into my tear ducts at once. Lying to be here. Being here. Being *here*.

I can hear Kareena laughing every time a door down the corridor is opened. I stand up and allow the tractor beam of my hero's laugh draw me towards the door.

It's too late to double back to where I've been left because the room she is in is glass-fronted and she is standing up, pacing around a table of about six white guys in a mixture of light blue shirts, checked shirts, band T-shirts, as they all read from their laptop screens and talk over each other. Kareena has her phone in her hand and occasionally pauses to write things down. She spies me through the door as I linger, wanting to be noticed, and she ushers me into the room.

I approach the door tentatively and Kareena skips the length of the table to open it for me.

'Welcome, welcome,' she says. 'This is the sweat box. Where I make all my writers sweat over which jokes of theirs I'm going to use tonight. When I'm not here, they have to tussle and fight for my affections. Meet them.'

She points around the room, introducing me to the two Dans – a writing partnership – a Stevie and a Steve and Daddy Joe and Paul. I wave at each of them, a twinkle of fingers, trying not to seem like a complete dork.

'We were just running through tonight's monologue before moving on to you, which is good timing. Want to hear what we have?'

I nod and allow myself to be pushed towards a seat near the front of the table.

There is an electricity in my mind right now. This is it, this is the moment that has made this trip worth it. I am in the belly of the writing beast. I am watching how comedy gets made. I am listening to them pitch jokes and punch jokes.

'OK, go,' Kareena says, pointing at one of the two Dans.

Dan looks around the room and raises his hands for emphasis, his elbows off the table, a pen pinched between thumb and index finger.

'So,' he says. 'We're starting with the bit on the new government policy on recycling. How they're recycling their opponent's election manifesto promises. Then we move to Kareena's bit about sorting the recycling. Her different jars for ex-boyfriend tears, white woman tears, her own existential dread tears. Tears tears tears. Through to the crying poll. One in three people cry for attention, that poll. Then the story of how she cried for attention to get that date . . .'

'Thank you, Daddy Joe,' Kareena says, pointing at Daddy Joe with her phone. She looks at me. 'It's how he met his current wife.'

Daddy Joe nods, holding his hands on the table, hunched at the neck as if he hadn't quite counted on sharing that story with the whole world.

'Then intro the actor, story about his most famous role, your impression, fun, fun, fun, and then intro Madhu and then the musical act, gridlock, and go . . .'

'And then begins the show,' Kareena says hopefully. 'Great work, everyone. OK, back to it, punch up those kill lines for me. And you know what? Move Madhu up to the top. That way everyone tuning in just to see that actor's cheekbones doesn't turn off. I'll be back, I'm going to take Madhu here for a little walk and get to know her.'

I stand up, expectantly. I am floating through this entire

experience. I want to be consumed by Kareena. Her presence sends shivers down me, electricity everywhere. I am never washing my clothes again. She side-hugs me and I can smell her again. This time the immaculate shea butter is mixed with the smell of coffee and sweat. But it doesn't matter. It feels so real to me. Everything in this moment feels like the realest thing I have ever wanted in my life.

What did I expect life to become if not this? How could I allow myself to talk about becoming a lawyer, for god's sake? That's not me.

I look around at the people moving for Kareena and I look back at the writers shouting lines across to each other over the table and I realise what my life needs to be.

Kareena pulls me down the corridor and points to pictures on the walls. It's her with different guests, actors, comedians, musicians. She looks so happy in all of them.

'I cannot tell you,' she whispers to me, 'how happy I am to have a brown sister on the show. It's been way too long.'

'I've never seen one,' I say, adding to the conspiracy.

'That's what I'm telling you, little sis. These people – they don't understand how underwhelming it is to be surrounded by a bunch of mediocre white people. You know, people hate to see me have this platform and kill it every single week. I see the tweets, the columns, the whatever whatever. Also, they hate how I'm making coin, innit.'

Kareena opens a door without a sign on it and leads me into what must be her office. The walls are adorned with tour posters. There are books and DVDs piled up precariously. A pleather sofa pointing at a television, a basketball game on pause. The room smells of unemptied bins and deodorant.

'Welcome to the lab,' Kareena says. 'I do all my thinking in here. It's my oasis away from them lot. Which is why it looks and smells like a teenager's bedroom.'

'It doesn't smell like my bedroom,' I say and Kareena laughs, almost as if she had forgotten the age gap.

I pick up a biography of Richard Pryor and flick through it. He's the master, apparently. I've never really listened to his stuff.

'You read that?'

I shake my head.

'Oh man, you have to read it. It talks about his early life and how it formed his comedy. Like, it tracks different routines to their roots and tries to understand where they might have come from. He was the master, for sure.'

'That's what I hear,' I reply, putting the book down. It feels alien to me. Because there is only one master and I'm standing in the recreation of her teenage bedroom.

'You don't know Pryor? My god, sis, you have to get to know. He's the one for me. The one who kicked everything off. The comedian who made it all seem possible. We all have one. If you're going to be a stand-up, you have to be into Pryor. He turned all his pain into amazing stand-up.' She laughs. 'But what do you know about pain? You're seventeen.'

'You don't remember being seventeen, do you?' I say,

pushing back and Kareena beams at me, like I've done something very right.

Kareena grabs the biography and a bunch of DVDs from a shelf, finding a tote bag branded with a skin care range I've seen on Instagram and wondered, why are you advertising this overpriced stuff to a teenager who barely makes minimum wage on her part-time job? She puts all the Pryor paraphernalia into the bag and thrusts it at me.

'It's a loan. I want them all back.'

I accept the bag and hold it by its straps, letting the light load fall to a dangling position. I stare inside the bag and smile at this gift, evidence of heroism. A kindness. She wants to see me again. This is amazing.

I have to tell her. I really have to do it. Now or never.

'You're the comedian that made it all seem possible,' I say, my eyes boring a hole into the tote bag. 'You. It's only ever been you.'

Kareena snorts.

'Mate, you need to do a comedy education course then. Because I am sick, I know, but I am nothing without my comedy heroes. I know, they're all dudes. But, you know, they didn't let girls be funny till a few years ago so I haven't got many girl heroes.'

'I heard you talking about . . .' I dither on whether to paraphrase her own joke back to her but in the end just do it. I tell her about how I discovered her, how I got obsessed with her, how I wanted to be her, everything.

She leans back on her desk, arms folded and listens, beaming. I can't tell if I'm being creepy or saying the right thing so I just assume it's OK because she hasn't thrown me out on to the street yet.

When I finish, I stare at her, my head pointed downwards, my eyes looking up like I'm a cute deer about to be murked in the face by an American hunter with a way too big shotgun.

'Well, what can I say? It's always nice to meet a fan. A creepy-ass fan. Jesus, stalker, wanna play PlayStation with me while I press the panic button and get security to get you the hell out of here?'

I nod, not quite sure if she's joking or not. I sit on the sofa next to her as she plops herself down, falling backwards, making a pleased *ahhhhhh* noise.

She looks at me and laughs, knowing I can't work out if she's playing me or not.

'No one likes sincerity in comedy, OK? Rule one. No one. I know I'm sick. You know I'm sick. You don't need to say it. That's why they say don't meet your heroes, cos a hero knowing they fundamentally changed the course of your life – it's a weird thing to hear, you know?'

I nod.

'Sorry.'

'Rule two . . . never apologise. OK?' She smacks my leg and pulls the bag from my hands, thrusting a controller at me. 'Right,' she says. 'Let's return the Bulls to their rightful place at the top of the game.'

She unpauses the game and plays. I stab at the controls with my thumbs, no idea what to do. But while I run around in circles and practise throwing and dunking, Kareena takes on the entire rest of the team herself and smashes up the scoreboard, dunk after dunk, three point after three point.

'So, tell me about growing up. You're from Bristol, yes? That's outside of London? I think I've heard of it. I'm only playing with you . . . I like the audiences in Bristol. They really come to see a brown girl to tick off woke points, so I like to always make them bristle a bit. Like, their expectation shouldn't be that I am the righteous female they expect . . .'

'Yeah, I was born and bred there . . .'

'Parents run a shop, right? I feel like you told our producers that.'

'Yeah, since I was born. Before that, they both worked at the car factory in Avonmouth.'

'Seen, seen. Man, yeah, you are exactly the stereotypical kid that all the brown people don't want to acknowledge exists. That must suck, that we spend so long pretending you don't exist so we can combat stereotypes and what not—'

'Turns out we exist . . .' I say, overlapping.

Kareena pauses the game and swivels to me, a knee up on the sofa, and smiles, pressing her controller to her nose.

'Tell me about your family,' she says. 'Maybe we can use them in the show somehow.'

'Oh, they don't know I'm here. They don't watch the show.'

'Where do they think you are?'

'Staying at a friend's house. They don't know this bit of my life. Wanting to do stand-up, all that stuff. They think it's silly. Not even a hobby. Just, you know, something else.'

'You're talking to the queen of this. Let me guess: law? Pharmacy?'

'Such stereotypes, aren't we? Every time I see another brown thing about strict parents wanting the goofy artist to do a proper job, I cringe,' I say. 'Partly cos it's hack. Partly cos it's true.'

'Innit,' Kareena says, laughing and rolling her head back. 'Listen, I know it all. The worst bit of the stereotype is when it's true and you'd rather people not know that. Like, why can't we also have the complexity to be Patels in corner shops and stuff, you know?'

'Yeah, my dad's hilarious, man. I love him so much and I get why he's like, life's been hard, get a foundation, a strong foundation, before, you know, going off to do whatever you want . . .'

'It's the immigrant dream. Give us the foundation our parents never had. You got an older brother or sister? Sister, right? I can tell. I bet your sis is the first to go uni, like I was in my family. I mean, look, uni is ultimately whatever, you know. But our parents saw that as the holy grail. I did my degree for them, and everything after for me.'

'No,' I say, quietly. Looking around the room, before settling on the basketball game, staring at my avatar, facing the crowd with his hands on his hips. 'Meena didn't go uni. She, like, yeah . . . decided she didn't want to go. She wanted to do other stuff.'

Kareena leans forward, touches my knee. I stare at her hand, her chipped black nail polish, the ring that says OG on it, the faded fine line pen notes across the back of it.

'Like what?' she asks, softly.

I feel like I want to tell Kareena everything. She'll understand my pain. I know she will. She has been through all of these things before. All her pain is there, in her comedy, she completely understands me and where I come from.

'She didn't know what she wanted to do, and so decided she would figure it out first and then decide about uni. And then she and her boyfriend decided they wanted a baby. So they had one, and Mum and Papa were furious. Acting like once she has a kid, her future is over, because it becomes about the kid.'

'I bet,' Kareena says. 'I bet.'

'But like, that's what she wanted. I know her boyfriend ended up deciding that he did wanna go uni in the end, and that was cool and everything. But the way Mum and Papa threw her out, cut her off,' I say, knowing that the tears forming in the corners of my eyelids are a year's worth. 'It's just so sad. So clinical. Like, bye-bye. Like, you want a kid, you're no longer a kid.'

'Man, that's so rough,' Kareena says. She leans forward and throws her hands out. I lean forward into her cuddle. My tears erupt on to her T-shirt and I try to say I'm sorry, but I'm so sad, and so embarrassed, that it makes my voice wail and crack, all in the same syllable.

'I haven't even met my niece,' I sob.

'Mate,' Kareena says. 'Look, if I can offer a bit of advice . . .?'

I nod into her T-shirt; her whisper is loud in my ear but I am hanging on every single word.

'Put it all into the comedy,' she says, before releasing me and holding me at arm's length. 'My god, you have the perfect story that is ripe for a ripping. Rip it apart. Find the tragedy. Make the tragedy funny. It's perfect.'

I know we've just met and yet here I am, spilling my guts on to her, my tears literally soaked into the threads of her clothes, ladies and gentlemen, and I feel all weird and vulnerable, but why would I want to talk about this stuff onstage?

'You're looking confused, but trust me . . . Comedy is like . . . better than therapy, honestly.'

Kareena springs off the sofa, like a basketballer leaping for the net across half the court. Before I can even move, she is on the other side of her desk, smiling, a pen in her hand, scrabbling around amongst papers and books, looking for something. She eventually pulls out an old exercise book, one you might have at school.

'This is the lab,' she says, shaking the exercise book at me.

'Did you rob a school?' I ask.

'Yes. Well, my sis is a teacher and nicks them for me. Dunno why, but I love filling these with my ideas instead of the posh expensive notebooks everyone buys me for my birthday because what do you get the newly rich person who has now filled her life with everything she wanted growing up?'

I stand up and look for somewhere to sit while Kareena grabs her swivel chair, hops into it and crosses her legs, removing her kicks as she moves.

I hover uselessly before resting on the arm of the sofa.

'Your dad, tell me about him,' Kareena says. 'What's his worst quality? Like properly worst quality. Apart from, you know, chucking your pregnant sister out of the family home.'

'I don't know,' I say, spirited away by the collusion with my hero on this. 'He forms his opinions based on the first thing you say. Like, if you say, "Papa, I'd like a chat", he assumes it's going to be something difficult and he prepares himself to say no, even if the question is, do you want an ice cream?'

Kareena nods. 'Classic,' she says. 'Classic Indian dad. Just somewhere else at all times . . .'

'Probably at work. Like he has mastered astral projections . . .'

'So his body's at home and quietly watching B4U . . .'

'And his mind is in the shop, doing a never-ending stock take?'

We both fall about laughing.

'Still, pretty harsh of him,' Kareena says. 'You know, chucking your sis out like that.'

'Yeah,' I reply. 'It was bad. All because she didn't do the thing he demanded she do.'

'Uni?' she says, like, *Of course*, shaking her head and

grimacing. I nod, because she understands. 'Same old, same old.'

'And anyway, what an utter privilege to be able to even consider uni as an option,' I say. 'Like, why is it so important nowadays? It's loads of debt and it doesn't even guarantee a job at the end, right?'

'How is your sis?'

I stand up, not wanting to answer Kareena. What do I even say? That I cowered and let Papa throw her out? That she could have stayed if she had offered the old-man-stuck-in-his-ways an olive branch, that they're both as bad as each other, and me and Mum, worse in our silence?

It was a mess. Because both Mum and I watched it escalate beyond repair, and neither of us stepped in to offer a route forward. I could tell, the day Meena left, that she was disappointed in me the most. I watched her and her boyfriend wheel out a suitcase, a box of her books and a few miscellaneous carrier bags of things. She left everything like it was a guest bedroom and she'd finished up a month at a distant uncle's house. She'd looked at me and gathered her hands around her belly. It really had started to show since the apocalyptic fight had taken place. I gave her sad, doleful eyes, like I didn't want things to be this way. I wanted to speak and I wanted to say something and I wanted to reach out and shout about how I felt and I wanted to tell them that they were both a little wrong, him more than her and it was their stubbornness that had turned the fight in this direction. But I stayed silent and watched and waited for her to leave, because the longer she lingered, the guiltier I felt.

In the days after she left, I kept forgetting she wasn't there and would storm into her room to tell her things and absentmindedly get cutlery out for her at dinner. Or, I *really knew* she wasn't there, and my fingers would hover over the send button for a one-word apology text, or I argued with Papa in my head.

Over the months, my relationship with my dad defrosted.

He took an interest in me that he didn't seem to have before, in either of us. He wasn't overbearing in his expectations of what I might do, instead he was just present for my decision-making, which pressurised me into making decisions that pleased him. Go to uni, the pervading mood of the house seemed to be. He helped me think through ideas for my personal statement, gave me ideas on which universities to apply for, even arranged for us to visit Birmingham.

Luckily, we were both thrown by the place. In the car home, Papa said, 'You might as well stay in Bristol. I couldn't tell the difference between the two.'

And then, finally, one night, Meena broke our silence.

She texted me to ask if it was appropriate for her to text me happy birthday and I replied, 'Of course'.

She texted me happy birthday.

It wasn't my birthday. It was a peace offering. We messaged back and forth and then I thought, oh god, I just need to hear your voice, so I called her. She declined the call, texting me immediately to say we weren't there yet.

That destroyed me.

I was staring at my phone, mentally drafting a text, unsure of what to say, when she texted again.

We are always going to be sisters. I say that to say this: we will find our way back to each other. I just need to sit with my anger for a bit. And you need to sit with your guilt. That's OK. It's painful.

Once we've dealt with this stuff, we can work our way back to acting like sisters instead of just being like hi how are you did you see that episode of that show did you hear the new single by remember when.

I cried at her response and replied:

I hear what you're saying. I feel guilty. And I miss you.

She replied:

Good. We'll speak soon, sister.

Since then, I've been desperate to talk to her, hear her voice, meet my niece. I wear it so heavily everywhere. Every square inch of me is consumed with this betrayal I made.

'Are you OK?' Kareena asks.

I shake my head, feeling the tears coming. She leaps over the back of the sofa, her hand on the armrest and she pulls me into her. The tears are full and tired and thick.

'Come with me,' she says.

14

I don't know quite what happens in the next few steps, but Kareena, with her arm around me, humming a Jai Paul song, leads me into a lift, presses her fob to a keypad, after fumbling it out from her hip. She presses the button for the top floor and we ride up, her arm still around me protectively, like she's never going to let go.

This is not how I imagined what meeting my hero would be like.

'I'm about to show you something cool.'

I nod; I can't bring myself to reply. I don't trust my voice. I don't trust how embarrassed I feel. I don't trust anything I am doing right now. For a fleeting second, I worry about Jazz but I know he'll have befriended the writing team and handed out the business cards he has had in his top pocket for years.

The lift doors open out on to a rooftop.

Kareena and I step out together and she releases me slowly before grabbing my hand and spinning me around in a circle.

'Look, I brought you up here to give you a bit of advice, a pep talk, a warning and a kick up the butt. All in the same speech.

Are you ready?' I nod, amazed that she is mentoring me in this way, giving me such generosity.

'Please . . .' I say.

'Does it matter whether my audience cares about you? Or whether I care? About you, your voice, your comedy career, what you do with your life. Nah. What matters is how much *you* care – about you, your voice, your comedy career, what you do with your life. OK? You need to care more than all of us combined. There are times you find yourself at the top of other people's priority lists. But you will always be at the top of your own priority list. You feel me? In the same way that I am the most important person in my career, no matter what good I do for others, I will always do right by myself first and foremost. And it's the same for you, OK? This may be difficult for you to hear because when I was your age, my ego was all about being noticed. Now it's about staying on top. So you need to pull yourself together, and not blame yourself for what happened in your family. And know that next time you need to speak, you will, because you've seen the consequences of not calling stuff out.'

I smile. I love her.

'Now, here's the warning. Every industry – comedy, lawyering, even uni, is filled with snakes who are also at the top of their own priority list. No one will ever give a damn about you more than *you* give a damn about you. Don't trust any of us.'

'Got you.'

'You don't. Not yet. You don't get me. But you will. I'll make sure of that. Now, here's the kick up the butt. I expect a good show. From all of you. Currently, I've got a boring Hollywood actor who just wants to promote their movie without me acknowledging the photos of them in blackface when they were at college. I've got gridlock, a musician who is half my age acting like I'm the least important thing in the world. And I've got the future of comedy, crying, cos she felt powerless to speak up against her dad when it mattered. Know what I'm saying?'

'Pull myself together?'

'Exactly, sis. Exactly. Now, look, think I do this for all my guests?'

'No,' I say, flicking hair hypnotised by the wind from my face. 'Thank you. It's really kind of you to spend the time.'

'It is, you're right, it is. And now I need to go and shout at my writers for not being as funny as me. Let's get you back to your boyfriend.'

'Oh,' I say, embarrassed, hands in pockets, foot crossed over foot, completely weirded out by the suggestion. 'He's not . . .'

'Oh, I know,' Kareena says, laughing. 'He just wants to be.'

She pushes past me, like she's not waiting around, and does not hear my protests about Jazz. I realise, in uttering his name, I wish he'd been given this pep talk as well. She heads to the lift. I follow her. Completely hanging on her every movement, wishing to drink in her presence for ever.

15

Jazz and I sit at a table in the staff room and wait. He checks his phone, silently. I can feel a tension in the way he sighs every ten seconds or so, like he's reminding me he's there, like I abandoned him or something.

'You OK?' I ask, smiling.

'Sure,' he says slowly, adding a further longer sigh, just for effect.

'I just had the best hour of my entire life just now. I mean, you wouldn't complain about that. I played PS5 with Kareena, she gave me career advice and I just feel like a changed person. It's awesome.'

We had taken the lift in silence, but I had that fizzing sensation in my legs, like I just wanted to erupt and punch everything and scream. Like I'd been lying as still as possible in a confined space for days and now I was ready to take on the world. I felt like I was invincible. Of course, Kareena was right. I had spent so long prioritising other people's wishes, especially Papa's – be a good child, be what's expected, the whole time – and I hadn't even taken a beat to realise what I wanted.

Also, Meena did what she wanted; why couldn't I? Why not me? Prioritise me. What a message. What a way to live your life. What a motto.

As Kareena had left the lift, she had looked at me, spudded me, her body stiff, then headed back to the writer's room. All business-like. Leaving me in the corridor of bustle, as television was being made all around me. I had breathed in the frantic caffeinated energy in full, a sumptuous buzz that clattered off the walls and sprung everyone's steps into methodical, frenetic action.

We were all in the service of this awesome woman. And as she had spoken to Hannah, now wearing a headset and carrying a clipboard, she had pointed in my direction and Hannah had approached me, beaming.

'Let's find you a home,' she had said, very enthusiastically, almost like she had been trying to distract me from a dead body in the conference room.

I had spied Jazz, loitering, on his phone, anonymously lingering, trying to look like he belonged there. I offered him an arm to link through as I passed, beaming from ear to ear from my audience with the queen – my bit of advice, my pep talk, my warning and my kick up the butt, all in the same speech; Kareena's words pinging between my heart and head, noisily. Jazz had pretended he didn't see it and walked a few steps behind me.

He didn't say a word to me until now, and I can feel some distance in the way he positions himself to me.

'Best hour of your life?' he says, sighing again. Then, flatly, 'Please. Do tell.'

'Listen, Kareena is a gangster,' I tell him, practically foaming at the mouth. 'She was just so kind to me.'

'Nice,' Jazz says, sounding hurt.

'Listen, man, I know you don't like her or whatever and you're just here to network and shit but seriously, she cares about me. She took care of me. I told her some deep stuff about my life and she gave me a proper pep talk about how to just get on with getting on. I rate that. She took the time.'

'Great,' Jazz mouths, his eyes not leaving his phone screen, which I can see from the glint in his glasses isn't even on.

'At least she's not pouting cos I went off for a little bit.'

Jazz looks up at me and shakes his head.

'That's not what this is about,' he says.

'What is it about? Jealousy? Come on, Jazz, you serious? You wanted an audience with the queen too?'

'Or maybe, I'm due my shot too. I didn't luck out into all this nonsense like you. I worked hard.'

'So what?' I say, placing my hands on the table, rising off the seat slightly. 'I didn't work hard? Is that what this comes down to? I worked hard for this therefore I am entitled to this.'

Jazz shakes his head.

'No, that's not it,' he says, his voice cracking, like he's about to cry. 'I want you to be here because you want to be here, not because of her. Because you want to be . . .'

'Am I interrupting?' someone says. I turn around to see

138

another checked-shirt-wearing, headset-chomping, clipboard-holding person.

'Hey,' she says, holding out a hand. I shake it. Her hand is cold and surprisingly small. 'I'm Hannah, here to do your pre-interview before the show. You OK to do that?'

I double-take at Jazz. Another Hannah. He breaks, despite the mood.

'Sure,' I say. 'Also, I just wanted to say thank you. I'm really happy to be here and I'm honoured to showcase my comedy on Kareena's show.'

'Oh,' Hannah says. 'Kareena's just had a word with the writing team and thinks it would be best if we do this as a straight-up interview now, instead of you doing a five-minute set. I suppose we can work in a couple of jokes though.'

I look at Jazz. He is purposefully not looking up from his phone.

'Oh, OK,' I say. 'Sure. I could do an interview. I mean, what's the worst that can happen?'

'Have you ever seen any movie ever?' Jazz says. 'Someone always asks what's the worst that could happen right before the worst happens.'

I nod at Jazz, like, *Sure, mate, sure.*

16

After Hannah has prepped me for the questions Kareena will ask, which are mild and fixated on the viral video (questions like 'Poor Marvin, what's he ever done to you?'), I am sent to have my make-up done, which involves a lecture about how I need to take better care of my skin by a stranger who is appalled by my lack of regime.

Next, I am taken to meet a sound engineer who mics me up and storms off when I point out the flesh-coloured microphone he keeps referring to isn't my flesh colour.

When I am taken back to Jazz, he stands as I approach and smiles. He has his bag on his back, his jacket zipped up. Real going-on-a-journey stuff.

'Listen,' he says. 'Good luck tonight. I really mean it.'

'You look like you're going,' I say. 'This feels like good luck and good night. Your bag is on both straps. Where are you going?'

'I think you have everything under control here,' Jazz says. 'I'm going to go write my joke at the cafe, hit up this open mic in Camden and then head home on the eleven thirty train. I'll see you on there?'

I get it. He didn't get what he wanted in coming so he's bouncing. Fair. All's fair, I guess. All is fair in love and in war and in stage time.

'Cool, man. Yeah, maybe see you on the train. Save me a seat, innit. If you find the time, get us a Maccy Ds,' I say, resigned, feeling suddenly like the loneliest person in the world.

'Right,' Jazz says.

He puts his hands in his pockets and shuffles past me, head down, back towards reception. I turn to watch him as Hannah repeats the time constraints we're under. I can't hear her. All I can hear is the flicker of the neon lights and the feedback from a microphone in a room far away that isn't mine.

'Bye then, soldier. Go get those comedy medals,' I shout after him. He doesn't turn back, just offers me a salute.

And then I'm alone. With Hannah.

'You OK?' Hannah asks. I nod. 'Good,' she says, her voice a little more steely now she knows I'm not bawling. 'Let's get you ready.'

I'm taken to what's called a green room, even though it's not green. It's basically a bunch of sofas on the other side of the wall to the studio where they record. I'm reminded that I'm the first guest so I need to stay in the room till after my recording.

As I enter, I can feel a dampness in the air, like everything muffles slightly.

'This room feels weird,' I say quietly to Hannah.

'It's soundproofed, so they can't hear us from the stage,'

Hannah says. She points to a television screen, which is flipping between four angles: Kareena's desk where she interviews guests, the guests' sofa, a wide shot of the whole stage and the audience. People are talking in quiet television babble to each other that I don't understand.

I see the actor and gridlock, taking up space in the green room, heads close together as they clutch bottled beers and talk. The actor is shaking his leg up and down. They seem like best friends plotting to steal one of their dad's cars and head to the coast to pick up chicks or something. It's so unreal how they look. I don't even give them the dignity of looking at them like they're real people.

I snort-laugh at how bizarre the situation is and the actor looks up, eyeing me till he realises I'm a nobody. Hannah doesn't even get a look in. It's like the headset and clipboard render her invisible in front of people like him.

'Want me to introduce you?'

'Sure,' I say. 'Pretend I'm, like, the queen of somewhere, Rajasthan. I bet they'll stop looking through us then.'

Hannah laughs.

'To be honest, I think they'd only notice you if you were more famous than them.'

'Who says I'm not?' I reply, defiantly.

I laugh again and gridlock looks up this time as well. He nods at me and is on his feet, approaching us. I look at Hannah, like, help, because he is suddenly in front of me, looking at me intently.

142

He plays acoustic-guitar sad songs, the kind of sad songs that play over the montage at the end of American TV shows, you know – when all the characters are having the bittersweet resolution to whatever they've been wrestling with that week. He is intense. Like he doesn't speak to many people and he really feels every emotion on his face.

He extends a fist to me to spud and I grab it.

'Paper beats rock!' I shout and Hannah laughs.

He looks confused, then smiles because he knows a joke has been told, even if he doesn't get it. The weakness in his armour of cool and sad exposed, I am off to the races.

'Listen, brother, it's interesting you offer me a daps, not a handshake or a high five. Is it so I don't damage your precious fingers?' He holds one hand in the other and massages it like I've caused him a world of pain. 'Bro, look, it ain't like that. I don't want you to be afraid. Yes there are two brown people in the building. I'm not Kareena. Or her sister, before you infer that. I'm just a nobody, innit. But thank you for saying hello. It's more than I can say for Mr Won't Win An Oscar there.' I can feel Hannah, clutching my arm, trying to remain professional, but also, like I need to stop, like also, she really needs to buss out into a heap of laughter on the floor. 'Yo, Mr Won't Win An Oscar, why are you always leaning with your back against whatever fit young girl everyone fancies this month? She's literally a prop for you. That's awful. The optics of that. Especially after all that "me too" stuff conveniently went away. But you go for your life mate. Anyway, I'm looking forward to the show, yes, yes, yes . . .'

gridlock stares at me intently, really feeling the impact of my words while the actor has gone back to his phone and is staring at it like he's just been offered a role on Broadway. Actually, probably just another romcom where he plays a much older man about to go out with a girl barely in her thirties.

I feel so me in this moment. Like I've been suppressing my best side for so long. And right now, I'm a powerful entity. You will listen to me.

This is my voice. My beautiful voice, beholden only to truth.

I've missed you, friend. You've been hiding away too long, scared of what people out there think about you.

'I liked that video of you slating that kid,' gridlock says. 'Now I know how he must have felt.'

He laughs and wanders off to pick up his guitar, lying down on another sofa and strumming it plaintively, singing, 'She rinsed me like she did Marvin' again and again.

'Well,' Hannah says. 'Help yourself to anything in the room except the alcohol and drugs . . .'

'Thanks,' I say, giggling. I had mentioned to her that perhaps it wasn't cool to let a couple of under eighteens loose in her building. But she legit can't just sit with me for ever. 'You get back to your job.'

With Hannah gone, the atmosphere in the room is strange. gridlock won't stop strumming his guitar. The actor is pretending to sleep but because he's a bad actor, he's over-the-top not-sleeping, like a seven year old pretending to be asleep at a sleepover when the adults come-a-checking.

Kareena bounds into the room after an indeterminate amount of time, during which nerves have crept all over my body and started banging cymbals over and over again, thumping and clashing through every part of me.

She's wearing her show uniform of black T-shirt and jeans with bright white canvas shoes. Her hair is down and gleaming now, moving in unison, wavy and shiny. She beams at everyone. The actor stands up and gridlock stands and strums, singing her name over and over again.

Kareena does the running man to the strum and looks at all of us.

'We ready, guys?' she asks.

'Definitely,' the actor says. 'Listen, what's with your sister?'

He points to me.

Kareena looks at me and laughs. 'Oh, I know we're brown but we're not related, sweetheart. Why? Did she destroy you like she does everyone?'

I've come a long way from making jokes about being agnostic towards dogs, I think. Then I remember I haven't done the reading homework for school tomorrow. Looks like I'm bunking off again.

'I know she's not your *sister*,' the actor says. 'I meant, like sista, with an a.'

Kareena looks at me and rolls her eyes before glaring, like, *Don't say anything*. I wait for her to reply to the guy's microaggression. She takes a deep breath and smiles.

'Right,' she says, flatly. 'The show's about to start. No bad swearing. Light swearing is OK. And also, this isn't just a come-on-and-promote-your-terrible-stuff show. This is the Kareena show. You're all just passengers.' We all stare at her; I'm revelling in the silence that follows. 'Great pep talk, Kareena,' she says, quietly, to herself. 'Really inspired the masses there.'

Maybe she doesn't want bad vibes before the show.

'Thank—' I start to say, before Kareena offers us all a peace sign and leaves the room through a door that leads directly to the stage. A door we have been told to not open, no matter how much we want to.

I feel stiff. I haven't moved in minutes. I don't want to do this. I can feel that familiar drying of my mouth, the forgetfulness that includes the entire dictionary, the emptiness of everything invade my brain again. And then the demons start chatting quietly in my ear. *Why are you so good at rinsing people off the top of the dome but all your pre-prepared material is so stale? Also, dogs are amazing, man's best friend, we all know it. And why aren't they letting you do your material? Why are you just doing an interview? Is it because you're not funny? Like, how will you ever be like Kareena? How will you get to her level? Especially if you're not doing any comedy. Maybe the lawyer thing is right for you? You can form an argument and you can keep a judge entertained with how you deliver it. You're essentially the plot of* Legally Blonde. *How depressing. That your story would be such a cliché. It's a good film and everything and it's a shame it never had a sequel. (Yes, we know it had a sequel but we say it didn't have a sequel because the sequel was, just, bad. You know? Indefensibly bad.) What we're trying to tell you, though, is that your path has been chosen for you. And no matter what you do next, all that matters is you stick to the path.*

I can hear the audience shuffling nervously in the next room, slowly.

Cripes. Look at all these people.

I scroll through Twitter. People are still using memes and gifs of me as reactions to things. The way I don't own my face any more sends a shudder down my spine.

People laugh as the warm-up comedian comes on the stage. I look up at the screen and see a young Black guy wearing all khaki, with a bum bag strapped to his chest. I recognise him from a few YouTube videos. He grabs the microphone looking serious and then makes a joke about how this is the worst immigration interview ever.

He smiles and everyone relaxes into a laugh. He's laughing because he understands the power structures at play. They're laughing because if he's joking about an immigration interview, he must have passed it with flying colours.

I watch him hype the crowd. He does all the audience work, asking them where they're from, what they do and he cracks jokes about their careers, puts them on the spot. The laughter is heady. Like, people have been waiting for this so much. He keeps telling them they need to act like it's 11 p.m. – five hours from now, when the show goes out – that it's a live recording and they are about to have the night of their lives. That's the energy they need to bring. When he gets them all to do a call and response thing, the actor gets up and turns the volume down on a knob underneath the television.

'I'm watching that,' I say to him, but he ignores me.

I stand closer to the television. I've never seen this type of crowd-work stand-up in action before. Only heard about it.

I can hear the response from the audience reverberating through the walls. It's filling me with excitement. Like my toes are willing me to just lift up from my core and then I can fly.

Before I can master the secret gift of flight, I hear the warm-up guy say Kareena's name and the crowd erupt into a church-like reverie of whoops and claps and cheers and Balle Balles as her intro music, a jaunty bhangra loop, pulses through the air. The volume on the television goes up and I hear the actor clear his throat in my direction, like I need to get out of the way.

Here we go. The dream, it approaches.

17

A few years ago, Mum fell off a ladder trying to get a box of crisps down from the top shelf of the stockroom and Papa rushed her to hospital. On the bus, no less. And it was up to Meena and me to run the shop.

We fell into an easy rhythm. I stayed on the till as bad cop, asking everyone, no matter how old they were, for ID. No matter what they were buying. Tin of beans? Show me your ID. Chewing gum? ID. Fags and lottery tickets? ID, ID, ID.

Meena took over restocking the shop after the Sunday morning rush that happens between 1 a.m. and 10 a.m. without fail in our type of shop: people either on their way home from the club or waking up the night after the club needing fizzy drinks, emergency loaves of bread and milk and crisps to heal their sore heads.

In a lull after lunch, with nothing to do (ignoring Papa's 'if you have time to lean, you have time to clean' edict), Meena crossed her arms over the counter in front of me and lay her head, cheek down, on the backs of her hands.

'How is this a life?' she said.

'It's not so bad,' I replied. 'You get to people-watch and

witness weird stuff. Like that guy who freaked out because we only had the juice with bits in it. Or that woman who bought a candle, a piece of string, some batteries and a Pepperami, like, isn't that a weird shop?'

'How so?' Meena asked, shifting so her forehead rested on the backs of her hands now.

'Like, she's going to tie someone up, having lured them in with a candlelit dinner.'

'Pepperami?' Meena says, snorting.

'No, the Pepperami is just a protein snack to keep her going while she preps the murder. She's not going to eat any of the food, it's laced with poison.'

'And the batteries?'

'Oh, that's for her remote control. She wants to load up all the eps of *Love Island* she recorded.'

Meena laughed. She raised her head to look up at me.

'You see the worst in people,' she said. 'I don't mean that in a horrible way. Just, you're able to see the darkness in people. Why is that?'

I laughed, unsure whether I was being insulted or not.

'At least I notice people,' I said. 'You just assume everyone is great until you have reason not to.'

'Yeah, what a horrible way to live your life,' Meena said, standing up and leaning on her broom. 'I see the best in people.'

'It's just leaving yourself open for disappointment,' I tell her.

'It's healthier than starting off disappointed. Like, isn't that exhausting, making us all earn your trust?'

Meena backed away, sweeping comedically, tongue out. I knew she was joking but it hurt. What was she saying? That I always saw the worst in people and that made it hard for me to trust anyone? Like, I've seen people take advantage of her, of Papa and Mum, I've had teachers make assumptions about me because of who they see when I walk into a room. I've seen friends fall out with other friends because they weren't able to get past how their views of the world differed. I've seen friends excuse racism and misogyny.

'That's not fair,' I shouted at her.

A man stepped into the shop, then hesitated in the doorway, looking between me and my sister.

'Come in, mate,' I said. 'It's fine. Did you bring any ID with you?'

His interruption meant we didn't finish the conversation until it was way past the moment to do so. Her comments took root in me and began a campaign of corrupting my every thought. I started to second guess myself, ladies and gentlemen. Like, am I judgemental? But what if I'm right too? Doesn't that justify being judgemental? So what if I am harsh? I found that I would think a thing about a person and then allow myself to argue, in Meena's voice, why this person wasn't the way I assumed them to be, and then they'd prove me right. I started waging war on my own beliefs in my head.

A few days later, we were waiting for a bus, going into town so Meena could meet her boyfriend and I could go and sit in a bookshop and read till she was ready for us to go home. Like I was picking the conversation up again, like a few days' gap hadn't happened, I said what I had been rehearsing in my head.

'Why see the good in people? That is begging me to be hurt and disappointed all the time. Who wants to go through life constantly hurt and disappointed? I can't control how other people are, but I can control how much I let them in. Most people are not worth the time anyway.'

'I guess,' Meena said, as the bus arrived. The ultimate diss, not even engaging with me.

Was it true? Was I always disappointed with people from the get-go? To this day, it still troubles me. Do I make them earn my trust? I don't know if I can be sure of the answer. You don't always sit and make pronouncements about the sort of person you are, like you have a voiceover in some saccharine American TV drama. You just are. To exist is to be you. And to be you is to know your mind, say your mind, speak it. That's who Kareena is and that's who I am.

I'm lost in this line of enquiry, unsure why I remembered that day, that argument, that accusation from my sister right now of all times, seconds before—

'She just said your name, twice,' I hear, and I snap out of my head, looking at gridlock, who is standing way too close to me for comfort but also leaning his torso back as far as he can so it doesn't look like he's a creep who has breached my perimeter. Instead, he looks like he'd rather be standing anywhere else but here.

'What?' I say.

He nods to the door, then grins sweetly. 'You're up . . .'

I look to the door, and sure enough, it's being held open by a member of staff in a checked shirt and jeans. Headset – check. Clipboard – check. Hannah? No, not all white people look the same – someone else – check.

She is ushering me through urgently. I walk through the door into the darkness, a curtained-off part of the stage.

I stand there as the door closes behind me. I feel the staff member shuffling about, whispering 'Ready' into her headset and moving to the side of me. I see the curtain start to move.

It's time.

18

I walk out on to the set and it's like being in a dream. It doesn't feel real. The set is made up to look like a typical Indian household, so for a second it's confusing cos this could be my Mum's house. There is that same varnished wooden coffee table in front of the pleather sofas we're going to sit on. Obviously the sofas have been cling-filmed. Kareena is sitting on the sofa already, looking over at me. The dinner table, where she does the bit with members of the public, is set with those white plates with a ring of small green flowers around their circumference and empty serving bowls, made to look like this is a family get-together.

The paintings on the wall are all prints of oil paintings of Mughals and their courts. I feel like I am somewhere so familiar – but it's weird because walking on this set doesn't feel the same as watching it on television. Mostly because, there is a ceiling-less black hole filled with equipment and a whole audience where a wall should be. I can't see them but I can feel them.

I freeze at the side of the set searching for Kareena, suddenly freaking out that there is a crowd there that the big bright lights are obscuring from view.

I try to snap myself into what is happening because I cannot stop staring at the set.

In what seems like a lifetime, I see two paths form in front of me. Like a weird multiverse superhero timeline sort of thing.

Path one is the chosen path, the expected path, the path of least resistance. I become the one child who did what was expected of them. I go to law school and I find it hard because I'm at Bristol and navigating all the posh Tories too dumb for Oxbridge. I decide I need to defeat these beasts. I team up with the two other unproblematic people of colour doing law, also from Bristol, also working class, also cool as hell. And we all buddy up, study together, do moot court together, write essays together, share textbooks, because, oh me oh my, them mans is expensive. And we all get 2:1s, which is great for us because no one even expected us to finish the degree. We all have interviews for the same barrister's chambers. This is when my plan really kicks in because I know in my heart of hearts, the one firm we all want, the one in Bristol, it only wants one of us; it'll only take one non-posh ethnic. And you know it's going to be me. I worked too hard to get here. I have everything to lose. And so do my rivals. But also, what I have that they don't, is an aborted stand-up comedy career, which helps with my charm. I ace the interview, get the job, they love me so much my starting salary is enough to retire my parents, move us all into a house in Clifton, I reconcile them with Meena, we all play with my niece. And I die, unhappy, alone, on the top-range Ikea bed, because I'm rich enough to afford it. My law firm makes me a partner in death, and my niece avenges my death, because we know Jazz has been poisoning my food for years.

Path two: I do this show, get famous, get back on Twitter, hone my one-liners, start hitting up clubs, start getting booked by all the well-meaning people who want to do better about their lack of ethnic womens, start crushing it. People are like, where do I know you from? And I'm like, dude, I was a teen television comedy genius star. I move to London, do a law degree in name only, get kicked out for non-attendance. By this point, it doesn't matter. Kareena hires me as her new comic foil on season four of her show. Because, four seasons in, it needs a format change in order to keep people interested, and anyway, she is all about bringing in new talent. I become the youngest guest-host of a popular topical comedy panel show. I knock it out the park. I'm surprised at how little it pays. I win the best show award at Edinburgh that year and my parents are there to watch me receive it. I've invited them because I want them to see me in my element. They stand awkwardly everywhere we go and I'm constantly concerned about whether they are having a good time. That night, to celebrate my win, I take them for dinner at a fancy restaurant in town, and Meena shows up, my niece in a pushchair, asleep cos it's late – I've been doing press. And I reunite my family. They all make fun of me for being all comedy god now. And I make fun of them for falling out when they should have been there for each other. We laugh and laugh and laugh. Till Kareena calls me. She's quitting the show. She's got her big Hollywood call-up. They want me to take the reins. This is my show now.

'Come, come join me,' I hear Kareena say.

I'm shaken back into the studio, and I realise that Kareena is standing in front of me, looking at the audience, pointing at me and laughing, pulling my elbow at the same time.

'Sorry,' I say, realising the moment I'm in is on a path that hasn't been selected yet.

'Come on, come on,' Kareena says, radiating a different energy from before. Like she keeps side-eyeing me then looking at the audience with an expression I can't quite see.

I realise, having watched the show, that I am now the butt of the joke. Usually it's me, the audience member, in on the joke with Kareena. But now it's me she's side-eyeing.

'Hi,' I say, trying to recover, falsifying some bravado. 'I'm from the future. I've come back in time to save you from an apocalypse. Come with me if—'

'Hey, hey,' Kareena says. 'I do the bits. Come and sit down, Madhu, so we can get to know you . . .'

The silence of the crowd is suddenly oppressive. I feel like I've been wearing my trainers for days and my sweaty, tired feet have melded with the canvas for ever. I let Kareena lead me to the sofa and we sit down.

'Now, Madhu,' she says, drawing my attention to her instead of the all-seeing eye of the main camera, which is bearing down on me like an obelisk masking the presence of the many audience members behind it. 'Tell us why you've been internet famous this past week.'

'Oh,' I say, suddenly confused. I thought we were going to talk about comedy. 'Some guy was being horrible to my friend, so I let him know about it. And cos everyone is always filming everything instead of experiencing it, it got filmed and put online – without my permission, can I just add – and yeah, people decided to take the opportunity to call me, a teenager, either a comedy genius or an awful person. And in some cases, if I was lucky, they were racist. And doubly lucky, when they were misogynistic too.'

'Wow,' Kareena says. 'I mean, you are part of the reason boys have it tougher than girls, it seems. A guy can't act like an idiot to his girlfriend without a girl telling him how awful men are . . .'

'I know, right, so—'

'Listen,' Kareena says, interrupting. 'I think it's best we just see it for ourselves and then put it to an audience vote. Did Marvin deserve it?'

'Wait . . .' I say, not sure where this is going.

The set goes dark and I see the video appear on the monitors. I haven't watched it all the way through. I can't quite look at myself. I hear my voice, I hear the rhythm of it. It sounds so much deeper than it sounds in my head. I sound like a rapper, snapping into staccato attacks. I lean over to Kareena and ask if everything's OK.

Without taking her eyes off the screen I'm on, she says everything is fine.

When the video ends and the lights go up, Kareena fixes her eyes on me and smiles, almost mischievously. I don't know what's going to happen; all I know is, I suddenly feel too scared to speak.

'What was going through your mind when you were watching that?'

'I dunno, it felt like someone—'

'What about poor Marvin, what was going through your mind when you were rinsing him? Were you thinking about how he felt? Were you angry at your dad?'

'Sorry . . . I—?' I start to say but Kareena keeps on talking. Looking at the crowd, opening her hands out to them like she's bringing them up to date, she says something that makes my jaw drop.

'You see, Madhu has trouble at home. Her dad chucked her teenage sister out for getting pregnant and naturally, Madhu is very Tupac about the whole thing. Me against the world, baby . . .'

'No, that's not—'

'Listen, I get it, we all take out our anger on other people. But listen, let's put it to the audience. Audience members, grab table tennis bats from under the seat. Hold up the red side for "Marvin did not deserve it", and green for "Hell yes, destroy Marvin" . . .'

The lights go up and I can see the audience again. They are

159

reflective of my nightmare. All white adults, staring at me, holding up table tennis bats. It's even-handed, a balance of both colours.

'There we have it,' Kareena says. 'Mostly red. Poor Marvin. Now . . . do you have anything to say to Marvin before we bring our first proper guest out?'

'No, I—'

'Well, the next few minutes are going to be awkward, because, please welcome . . . the victim! Is that fair? To call him a victim . . .'

Don't do this don't do this don't do this don't do this . . .

'Marvin Taylor . . .'

Marvin walks out with the confidence of a man who just had the last six photos in his IG grid liked by his secret crush. Unstoppable. The fragrant whiff of validation turns these men into strutting peacocks, calling out for more attention. His arms are outstretched, messianic, with his fingers flickering up and down, welcoming the rapturous applause that greets him. How on earth did I become the bad person here?

I watch him walk on to the stage and stand facing me, arms folded. I look to Kareena for guidance, an explanation.

'Marvin,' Kareena shouts over the applause. 'Tell me, how did it feel? Having your life put on blast like that?'

'I'm not going to lie,' Marvin says, smiling widely, like this is going to be the big high point of his memoir. 'It was a tough moment to live through. I'm just glad I have this opportunity to have Madhu give me what I deserve . . .'

'A kick in the teeth?' I say, without thinking.

I expect a laugh. But I get nothing. Silence. Marvin shuffles about. Kareena is holding her hands to her face, in mock shock. I look at her, like, what is she doing?

'Look,' Marvin said. 'I understand you're going through a tough time with your family and everything. And clout is very important to you, Mads, but seriously. Trying to take a good guy like me down a peg. I ain't the problem.'

Kareena stands up and puts her arm around Marvin. She beckons for me to stand. I do, slowly, unsure, nervous. My palms are weak, knees are sweaty. Eminem got it mixed up.

'So,' Kareena says. 'I think the best thing to do here is say sorry to Marvin for humiliating him on the internet for clout.'

'Are you serious?' I say.

This is not how this was supposed to go. This is neither of the paths I saw. People will be watching this in a few hours. She's put my family business out there. She's made me say sorry for something I don't need to say sorry for. She's taken the comedy from me.

When this goes out tomorrow, people will know the truth about me: I don't deserve any of this.

I say sorry and Marvin cuddles me and the rest of the segment becomes a blur. I don't even remember saying anything. As soon as we break for an advert, Marvin is led off stage and I stand up to go.

Kareena springs to her feet. She has her arms folded. She is stiff and serious.

'Listen, can I give you some advice?' she says.

'I can't believe you did that to me,' I say quietly. I want to say more but I do not dare.

'Good, then heed the advice. You want to be a comedian? You need to be confronted by your fears. You get me? I took the power from you and your story on purpose. I wanted you to see that real comedy is tragedy. Is humiliation. Is pain. It's not rinsing people. I gave you so many opportunities to rise to the challenge tonight. And you failed. You failed utterly. You have a lot to learn.'

'Is that your advice?' I say, walking away. 'Great pep talk, coach. Have you ever thought of starting your own suicide prevention line?'

Kareena grabs my arm, actually grabs it, and spins me round, like I'm her daughter in a Hindi drama. Except I don't spin round in slow motion for ten minutes. I wrench my arm away from her, turn away and just keep walking.

'I showed you pain tonight,' she shouts after me. 'Learn from it. I helped you tell the truth. I don't need another brown comedian doing all the same jokes as everyone else, about buses being late and weird snacks. I want you to bare your soul on stage.'

I stop and turn back, hoping against hope my face is steely, not seconds away from crying.

'Isn't that my decision?' I ask. 'Why do we only get to talk about pain? Why can't I make jokes about buses being late and weird snacks?'

'They won't respect you unless you show them your pain,' she says, a clarity in her voice.

'That doesn't feel right to me,' I reply before walking away.

I push past the staff member into the green room. I'm greeted by the sight of Marvin charming the actor and the musician, his older brother in the corner, phone plugged into the wall as he scrolls idly.

Marvin, the actor and gridlock all look up at me. Marvin grins, gridlock offers a thumbs up and the actor, he looks through me.

I pick up my bag from under a chair, and my jacket, and I walk to the door.

'Hey, where are you going?' I hear Hannah call after me, but I ignore her; heading, as quickly as I can, to the fresh air of the outside world. The world I belong to. Not this utter mess.

19

I am angry. I am so angry. I am so very angry that I lose my way to the tube station, without Jazz to help me. I am so angry I can't even unlock my phone to call him or send him a message. I walk the streets and then I'm by the river and I realise I'm the stereotype of that idiot from outside of London who gets lost the second they arrive.

And that makes me more angry.

I spiral as I walk further and further into a London I don't understand. I forget which side of the river I'm on so I walk east thinking I'm walking west.

Kareena tried to teach me a lesson. On national television. About what? Resilience. Comedy is pain. Comedy is tragedy. Comedy is personifying and owning your trauma and humiliation. What a load of rubbish. She was the powerful one there. She had the opportunity to bring me through, another young brown person. And she just reduced me to nothing. For laughs. For the audience to laugh at me, at my family, at my rage at this guy who is objectively wrong. He cheated on my friend. I don't say sorry to someone like him. How dare they even suggest that this is something I need to do. And to put all my family's stuff out there for the public to judge? It destroys me. How dare she?

What was she trying to teach me? To know my place? To know that she's the boss? Was this, like, a power move? I'm the only funny brown girl; you can do something else? Was it an actual lesson? Like, learn from this.

But what did I learn?

That my hero sees me as competition, so I should see everyone as competition? That people can't distinguish between tragedy and humiliation? That no one asks your permission before filming you and putting it online and giving it to the social media gods to do what they will with it, and if you go viral, you no longer own your voice? That comedy is not for me?

I am lost.

I am lost I am lost I am lost.

Wait. I am actually lost, ladies and gentlemen. I lean on the railings and look out at the water and I look at the time. It is 11.27 p.m. I have wasted a good few hours on a self-pity spiral walk. You know the ones, where you walk aimlessly but fast, and run through every iteration of what you could have and should have said till you're arguing with ghosts in your head. And now I've missed the train. I don't know what to do.

I call Jazz, panicked. He doesn't answer. I look around at the street; there are no cars going past. No obvious taxis. Not that I have cash on me to pay for one. The studio was going to put me in a taxi back to the station because it was going to be tight.

I am screwed, man. So screwed. Stuck in a strange city overnight.

With no clue what to do, I stare out at the water, watching the reflective solidarity of a million tiny lights meeting in the shine of the murky water. I watch people on the other riverbank walking hand in hand, laughing and talking. I watch cars take people to where they need to be.

I watch another world pass by. One that does not belong to me.

I pick up the phone and note the time, cringing, knowing it's late, knowing their circumstance, knowing that we haven't spoken in so long.

I phone the only person who can help me right now.

20

The Uber that arrives to collect me is black and sleek, with tinted windows – so sturdy and posh, I'm initially confused it's even a taxi. Why would you own such a peng car and want to drive people around all day as they sit in their own filth? And other people's filth? The driver is bumping M Huncho. I get in on his side of the car and he is sitting so far back, my knees crunch against my stomach as I contort myself to fit in the back seat of the whip.

'Meena's little sis, yeah?' he asks.

'Yeah, how did . . .'

'She added a note to the pick-up. You know, you're lucky you have a big sis to bail you out like this.'

You don't know me, I want to say. But I realise, maybe Meena was right, I give people a hard time right from the get-go because I expect them to disappoint me. I give them no time and space just to be themselves and I take that for what it is, not for what I expect it to be.

Imagine: humbled by national television. I switch my phone off, I don't want to be contactable once the show is on.

The driver lets me stew until we approach the street she

lives on. I have stared at the front of her house on Google Street View many times before. It looks different at night. It's off a chaotic concourse of revellers coming and going from bars, standing out in front of bars, drinking, laughing, queuing for kebabs on their way home, leaning against darkened closed shop fronts with others, bodies intertwined, cavorting.

So much cavorting.

A quiet, subtly lit residential street. The driver slows his car and stops in front of number 23. I know this is her house because I asked for her address when my niece was born. I never sent anything.

'Thank you,' I say to the driver.

'Thank your sis too,' the driver says, and I stop myself from demanding he stop patronising me.

We don't know each other and he's right. I just don't need him to tell me.

I extract myself from the car and stand up in the street. The air is fresher and calmer here than where I got lost.

My sister is standing in the doorway of her place. She is dressed in her Brooklyn Nets vest and some grey gym shorts and she is barefoot, thumping her right leg up and down, like she does when she's nervous. She looks like exactly the person I would call my sister. She looks exactly the same.

I smile at her and call, 'Hey sis.'

She shushes me and ushers me into her home. I enter the hallway and close the door behind me, following her down the corridor to her flat. The door is open and I can hear a television playing an episode of *The Office*.

The flat is chaos, bottlenecked into a tiny space. The main room, no bigger than her bedroom at home, is part kitchen, part lounge. The television is in the corner, playing out the sitcom. Baby things are strewn everywhere. The kitchen is filled with dirty dishes. The place smells like burnt toast and hot milk.

'You didn't give me time to straighten up, sorry,' Meena says. 'Want a tea?'

I nod and stand in the liminal space between kitchen and lounge. My sister has aged. I know she's had a baby in the last six months and also a break-up and also I haven't seen her every day of my life like I did when she was at home, but she has aged. Her hair, tied back, is exploding out of a humble hairband's hold. She sighs a lot as she moves about the kitchen. And for someone who spent the years I knew her laughing at absolutely everything, she has a very serious face on.

I look around the room, desperate to see my niece.

'Where is . . .' I ask.

'Your niece? Kavita?' Meena says, one hand on hip, the other holding a filling kettle under a noisy tap. 'She's asleep. In the other room. Saeed is with her.'

'Saeed? You're back with him?' I try to not express too much shock.

'Yeah, is that a problem? Sorry, I thought it might be better than raising a kid by myself.'

'Sorry,' I say.

I watch as my sister stands by the kettle, holding on to the handle as it boils. She stares at me. I want to tell her everything. I want her to ask me. Because if she asks me, that means she still cares.

'Herbal or caffeinated? I'm having caffeine, I'm doing the night tonight. With the baby.'

'Me too, then. I can stay up with you and we can catch up.'

'The first train from Paddington's around five a.m. You'd need to leave here around four to get there on time. There's a train station across the road . . .'

'Something bad happened tonight, sis. Something real bad.'

'Oh,' Meena says, pouring water from the kettle into two mugs. Her other hand hasn't left her hip since I arrived. Like it's becoming a barrier between us. I cannot see past it. She pauses then looks at me. 'Something as bad as being chucked out of your home by your parents when you tell them you're pregnant?'

'All right, you don't need to go on about it. We all get it. You were pregnant. It's not like you created life or anything.'

Meena smiles. A whisper of air escapes her mouth. I have her.

'I mean, define bad,' I say, feeling the bounce return to the rhythm of my voice. 'Because you know when people on reality shows have to make decisions about who to fire or vote for to leave the show, and they're like, I feel so bad, this is the toughest thing I've ever had to do, I'm like, really? This is tougher than scaling a rockface without equipment, or telling a patient they have terminal cancer or eating popcorn without it getting stuck in your teeth for days? Really? This?'

Meena laughs. A hand over her mouth. She puts down two mugs of tea on the counter, steam framing the air between us. She pushes one to me.

'I've missed you,' she says.

'That all it took for you to forgive me? Comedy? Cos I have a heap of jokes raring to go.'

Meena sighs.

'I never blamed you for not having my back with Papa. You were young. I'm not mad about that,' she says, picking up her tea and blowing across the surface of it.

'What are you mad about?' I ask, mirroring her with my own mug.

'What's going on? Why are you stranded in London?'

I take a deep breath and tell my sister everything.

The story takes about ten minutes, and we move from leaning across the counter of the kitchen to sitting on the sofa, side by side but straining our bodies around to face each other as much as possible. I tell her about Kareena, and Marvin, and going viral, and Jazz training me to do stand-up, and the show at LOLZ, and the show at Hidden Corner, and the TV show, and how Kareena was super nice to make me feel all vulnerable and special but it turned out it was to soften me so the bit where she made me confront Marvin would be funnier and she could use more of the moment to make me look like the bad guy. Meena admits she missed all of this: new-borns and being up-to-date with what's trending being mutually exclusive.

I tell her about losing faith in myself and my voice. I tell her about how Papa wants me to do a law degree. I tell her about filling in my university application form and sending it off before I came. I tell her about my life being over.

She listens and she smiles when I exaggerate and she raises her eyebrows, bowing her head ever so slightly when I tell her about my feelings of inadequacy. And then I'm done. And instead of crying or shrugging, I say, 'Ladies and gentlemen, goodnight.'

Saeed appears in the doorway. He looks tired and frazzled and the baby is in a sling, writhing about, and my sister stands up and pats me on the shoulder and goes into the doorway, slipping an arm around his waist and her free hand on the top of Kavita. And I strain to see my niece but the door is closed behind them, and I hear their whispers and I sit in their flat and I feel like a stranger.

I am a spare part in my sister's new life.

21

Meena wakes me when it's time to get the train and I feel dizzy. Like I'm going to fall over. But she has called me an Uber and packed me a tea in a takeaway cup. She tells me to keep it. She hugs me like we're acquaintances at the wedding of someone neither of us know very well and walks me to the door.

I'm so sleepy I do all of this on autopilot. It's not till I sit in the taxi and gather myself and sip the tea, which jolts my senses back into the living, that I realise I didn't even properly meet my niece.

I sleep the entire train journey back, and I sleep on the bus, getting off a stop early because I'm so confused. And then I sleep in my bed.

When I wake up, it's dark outside. Saturday night is having to go on without me.

'Come in,' I say. A light tapping on the door has woken me.

Mum appears, with a plate of toast and a tea.

'Are you unwell?' she asks.

'No,' I say, sitting up, feeling like I haven't slept in weeks. 'Just tired.'

'I realise you are now perhaps at the age where I cannot ask where you've been. And I probably don't want to know the answer. So, just tell me everything is fine and I will make something up for your father.'

'Is he angry?'

'Neither of us knew you didn't sleep in your bed till this morning when you were late getting up.'

The light from the street breaks into fragments across my blanket, through fissures and tears where I have folded the curtains over each other to keep the world out.

I grab my phone and look through my notifications. There have been a lot since I got back home. I didn't check anything last night after the recording. I put my phone on airplane mode the second the Uber Meena called arrived. I didn't want to know about the reaction to the show when it aired later.

I thought about it on the train but sleep came to my rescue.

I thought about it when I got in, but it was too early to run the kettle. I got into bed and slid the phone off airplane mode, plugging it in. As I waited for the notifications to come through, sleep came to my rescue.

'Sorry,' I say to Mum, hoping it sounds like nothing more needs to be said.

I can feel my feet burning underneath the blanket. I'm wearing socks in bed like an absolute idiot. I reach down and push the socks over my heels before dragging them off. Free, my toes feel like they've been air-washed.

Are you OK?

A text from Shanai saying she just saw me on telly. She goes on to say she can't believe I said sorry to Marvin. She also can't believe what Kareena said about my family. She texts again if I'm OK. Hours later.

I'm hungry. And I need caffeine.

'Just tell me it was nothing I need to worry about,' Mum asks.

A text from Jazz asking if I got home OK cos he didn't see me on the train.

'Totally,' I murmur. 'Won't happen again.'

As Mummy Dearest puts my recovery kit down on the desk next to my bed, an old exam desk that was being thrown out because it had unredeemable swearwords carved into it, I see a notification from Marvin.

That was wild where u at?

I open WhatsApp and see he has followed up the text with a photo of him and Kareena in the green room. They're both grinning, him like he has finally discovered what it means to be alive and her like it's her last obligation before she heads out the door.

The final text from him says:

Kareena thinks u mad w us. Y tho?

I block him and cry.

Sometimes you need to cry – right, guys? Sometimes that thing inside you, it feels like a piece of bubblegum stuck to the curve of your heart and the only way to shift it is through tears.

Sometimes there is such a release in a good old-fashioned cry. It's a proper therapeutic cry when you're doing a person-wailing-and-throwing-their-body-over-the-coffin-before-it's-committed-to-the-flames crying. A silent cry is like a palate cleanser, a piece of lemon sorbet between arguments to clear the air. The mid-cry, when you need to wail but you want to be as quiet as possible – that's a frustrating cry. Usually it's when someone else is watching.

Right now, I'm doing the silent cry. Occasionally, I open my mouth and make a quivering sigh. I'm quiet and lying down on my side.

I can see Twitter notifications flash on my screen, tagging me into a clip from last night. I can't even watch it. How awful that this exists for ever now. Me being publicly thrown under the bus by my hero for laughs.

I can't look at them.

I feel empty. I feel bleak. I can see myself in the mirror, lying on my side, staring at myself.

The catastrophising has started, ladies and gentlemen. Look, I'm telling you this to be honest. I don't really want to admit it in public. But this feels like my worst thing that has ever happened to me. In a way that I understand and also don't. Like, I had my biggest opportunity yet to decide who I wanted to be snatched away from me by the person whose star shone so brightly she led me towards that decision. And I have no control over how people see it. They will see me as the angry brown girl going on television to defend something spurious like her misandry. Which we all know is rubbish. But I can't control how people will be. It's the worst thing. Everything feels over. I am never moving or leaving this bed again. The tea has gone cold, probably. The toast has gone soggy on the side in contact with the plate, probably. My socks are lost in the vortex of the blanket for ever, probably. Mostly because my mother is scarily obsessed with the hotel tuck. Like, I'll make my bed and then she will tuck all the edges in as tight as possible under the mattress. Even if I'm in there. She loves it. I hate it. Being constrained in the shroud of my blanket, it feels like I'm dying.

Today, right now, that feels OK.

Wishing to externalise my pain, I scan through the notifications. They are thick and fast. People calling me all sorts of names, accusing me of all sorts of things, everything between hating men and being a reputational terrorist, whatever that is. People make all sorts of convoluted assumptions on my upbringing. The notifications have come in a thicker, fuller, more vicious volume than when the video of me went viral.

If I do anything at all, I lose, I lose, I lose. But anyway, the true sadness of all of this is, I sort of believe what they all think about me.

Kareena didn't even care. She said she wanted to help me. She said she cared. She didn't care.

I feel voiceless in all this. Everyone has something to say about me but no one wants to hear from me. I feel like I'm swimming through thick muddy water, while a lasso pulls me back to shore to face the music. I feel so cloudy I'm throwing out bad similes that would make my GCSE English teacher happy. He was an idiot though. Wore comedy ties to work. Said Harvey Weinstein deserved a chance at redemption. Reckoned George R. R. Martin was a better writer than Jane Austen. Not sure where I stand on the last one; I have no skin in the game other than hating when people make it their personal mission to say popular culture has more literary merit than a classic without acknowledging that two things can be true at once.

I never realised the freedom I had to speak my mind until yesterday. I took it for granted. I didn't acknowledge that the freedom was conditional. Like, I didn't have the freedom to tell my dad how I felt about the way he treated Meena. And I didn't feel the freedom to demand that Kareena do better. But other times, most of the time, when I've spoken back, or spoken up, or just spoken, it's because I've never given myself pause to work out whether it's appropriate or not.

It makes me reflect on the fact that I've never spoken up when it really mattered, and that's what I should have worked on.

It's too late though, isn't it?

I hope I become the type of lawyer who speaks truth to power; who speaks up for the powerless, for whom justice is too expensive; who speaks to people like they deserve the space I hold.

I hope for all of these things, because this is my future now.

* * *

Sleepless, in the early hours and I stare at Twitter. I can't bring myself to delete my social media. And I can't bring myself to stop looking. I go on Kareena's Twitter, and she is retweeting all of the videos and comments about me, all the memes. She's not really commenting, just retweeting, which to me feels the same as endorsing them. I notice she has unfollowed me as well.

Angry, I go to send her a DM. I look at the last message we exchanged. When she said she was excited to meet me. A big 'X' at the end of it. I don't know what to say to her, so I throw my phone on the pillow.

It's enough to rouse me from bed. The humiliation. The rejection. The unfollowing. I stand up and practically fall on to the wall where her tour poster is. I rip it down, the corners staying tacked to the wall. I scrunch it up in my hands. I find my bin, and I shove her stupid face into it.

I grab my stack of comedy books and albums and pull them from the shelves above my desk. I throw them on the bed and run to the kitchen, where Mum is rolling out parathas. She doesn't really stop to look at me or what I'm doing. I grab a black bag from under the sink and run to my room. I shake the bag open. It takes a few beats longer than it should because I am rushing and I am possessed. I pick up the stack of comedy material and drop it into the bag. The corner of a particularly sharp book, probably a 'how to write comedy' guide, catches my big toe on the bone and I shout in pain. I shove everything I can into the bag, everything that resembles comedy.

I find some sandals and shove my feet into them, dragging

the black bag behind me, like it's got a dead body inside, one I've been trying to murder for a while, and I walk to the front door of the flat.

Outside in the corridor, I pull the black bag down the stairs, the books and CDs slapping the concrete of each step behind me. And when I reach the front door, I open it.

The outside world with its fresh air – somewhere, not here in this city, somewhere up there in the clouds – is disarming. I breathe deeply. I don't even say goodbye. It's like I have an ex who, boy oh boy, they did me wrong and I need to rid my space of every trace of them. They didn't cheat on me, they weren't mean to me, they just never fulfilled me, and then they betrayed me by making me realise how unimportant to them I was. One of them exes. Goodbye, comedy. It's not you, it's me.

Also, it's you.

Be gone.

I slam open the lid of the general waste bin and shout, 'You're not even good enough to recycle,' at the bag and I pull it up over my shoulder, and the binbag of comedy swings over my head and into the bin.

I close it and breathe.

I'll see you in court, I think. It doesn't make sense, but I realise, in my head, as I narrate this scene, I need one of those lines that people say to themselves in movies, that only people in movies say because they know there's an audience – something vague and empowering and stupid.

'I'll see you in court,' I say, out loud this time.

My heart is pounding, resuscitating me, bringing me into a world where everything has changed and I know who I am and what I'm about.

22

You know those movies and TV shows about lawyers where the lawyer has figured out how to win the case, or they've stumbled on the key bit of evidence that's going to nail the other side, and they stomp down the corridor, while a pumping song plays. Depending on the tone of the show, it could be like a big rap tune. Slow-motion walking to 'Ante Up' by M.O.P., or something like that.

I literally put 'Ante Up' on as I walk into college on Monday. I put the volume up so the thundering beat and the shrieking voices in my headphones give me tunnel vision. I only have eyes for the front doors.

I'm not so self-important that I think people will be noticing me and talking about me. I don't want to give anyone that space. I know people saw the segment. Marvin would have told them.

I present to you my case, Your Honour: I just want to get everything done that I need to, finish college and earn some money and head to university. Be the first. Be the one my parents were promised in exchange for their migration. Be the point of their sacrifice.

I spot Shanai sitting on a bench with Marvin, sharing

earbuds, laughing at something on screen. I can only assume it's me who is the object of their mocking. I do a double-take, like, what? I know I haven't replied to her text message and I know she saw us on television. A weekend is a long time when you're turbulently in love, I guess. I smile at her and she nods at me.

I reply to her text.

Funny seeing you two back together. What did I miss this weekend?

I see reply bubbles and turn back to look at her; she stares at her phone, thinking of what to write, and when Marvin kisses her neck, she puts her phone away.

I see Pri drinking coffee with Mark and Mel, laughing about something, and feel left out even though we don't really hang out unless we're with Shanai. I can only assume they're mocking someone. And that someone is me. Pri doesn't even go to college. I'm too busy ante-ing up to work out what on earth I've just witnessed.

I see my history teacher stomping across the grass, a wry smile on her face. I can only assume she's seen the video and is glad the kid in her class who has an answer for everything has finally had her comeuppance.

Me, me, me. They're all talking about me.

'Ante Up' hits a reload and I take a deep breath. Strictly business, I enter college through the main doors and look for my classroom. I will be the first to show up. I have a lot to say.

* * *

At lunchtime, I switch my phone on. I've deleted all social media. I scroll through WhatsApp. A lot of reaction texts from the last few days. I haven't been checking any of them. So I didn't see a text from Meena, from yesterday morning.

I open it and all it says is:

Why is Kareena Patel talking about my business? How does she know my business? Is this funny to you? Is my life something for you to laugh at? I am so disappointed. Don't contact me for a bit.

In one message, my sister has pulled the lawyer's robes from my body and reminded me, reminded the world, that I am not fit for any sympathy.

I hate myself.

My week gets worse and worse. My shift that Wednesday goes bad. I keep running through replies in my head. I texted a thorough sorry to Meena two days ago, after I read the text, and I'm still on one tick. Not even delivered. She has blocked me. I consider calling or texting or emailing it but if she has blocked me, she has blocked me and I have to respect that.

I put one of my favourite black T-shirts down on the kitchen table, not realising it's slick with sunflower oil from where Mum has been cooking. A big greasy streak all across the front. The T-shirt is ruined.

When I turn up to my shift, it's very busy. Surprisingly busy. And because my head and my heart aren't in it, I mangle orders, forget allergies, misplace drinks, neglect to charge a party of six, who slip away into the night, richer and full of free pizza. Everything goes wrong. When Danny says goodbye to me, he doesn't even have a nice thing to say about my shift other than to thank me for turning up on time. That much I managed. That's how low the bar is.

I walk to my bus stop but keep on walking past it, heading towards Park Street, to begin the slow decline into the centre of town.

A ruined favourite T-shirt. My sister hates me. For the triple, my self-loathing leads me to LOLZ. It's open-mic night and I can hear a ruffle of laughter from outside.

I poke my head in and see Leila, leaning on the counter, head inside her phone. I can see the stiff pacing presence of Jazz at the back. Maybe he senses me, like in movies where you just know the person is there, and he looks over towards the door. Part of me wonders why he hasn't reached out to me this weekend, but that same part knows I haven't reached out to him. I poke my head immediately out of the door and head towards another bus stop that will take me home.

I'm almost willing him to run out of the venue and shout after me and ask if I'm OK, and I almost know for certain I would cry on him if that happened, and I'm probably lucky, as is he, that he doesn't. Maybe I just want a friend.

I catch up with Shanai on the bus home. We talk about everything other than the thing and then as we are a stop away she leans in, grabs my arm and says, 'So, me and Marvin worked it out,' and I reply with some sort of faux 'Yay'.

'It's because of you. Thank you.'

'What do you mean?'

'You showed humility on that TV show, and it made me realise – he's a silly boy, but he's my silly boy.'

I tell her I don't understand and she says I don't need to, thanks me again and gets off the bus.

Shanai and Marvin are back together. That's a weird thing to think about.

When I reach home, our flat is in darkness. Oddness abounds. I prep myself for the next statue to fall in my crumbling mausoleum of dreams. I wonder what it'll be. Has Papa seen the show? Does he know I stayed with Meena? Did UCAS take one look at my application and think, this girl has no chance. Let's void the whole process and save everyone some time. Or, a hat-trick of all three?

I bet you're nervous, right, Your Honour?

I'm absolutely terrified, massaging my stomach as I stare up at the flat. Usually, all the lights are on. I have this stupid joke where I go around turning off the lights in unoccupied rooms, shouting, 'It's not Diwali', trying to single out the culprit. And when I have a shift, Papa always leaves the lounge light on for me to welcome me home, without fail.

Papa would have said if he saw the show, he's not really one to keep things to himself. I don't know why I want to tell him, I just know I have to. My stomach is doing that thing where it's hungry and full all at the same time, and it's churning like when

186

a printer gets jammed and the paper is pleading for release.

I get my keys out and take a deep breath, ready to face the consequences of my actions. I have nothing left to lose, I suppose. Might as well make absolutely everyone hate me.

The flat is dark and still when I enter. No life. No breathing. No lights. No ambient television. No stale milk smell from evening chai. None of it.

If Papa saw the show I am in so much trouble, I might as well not bother with university, cos I'll be too grounded to go to any lectures. I want to tell him first rather than risk him catching it unprepared. That way I can control the message.

I walk through the flat, unnerved, turning on all the lights that I can find, terrified this is all part of some horrific game where they jump out and shout at me. There is no one in the kitchen, main room, any of the bedrooms or toilet. I don't know why part of me is expecting a surprise zombie attack when the easiest thing to do is just phone my mum or papa. Papa's phone doesn't even ring once when I do call, but the voice that answers isn't his. It's something croaky and weak and female.

'Hello?' it asks. 'Madhu beti?'

Why is Mum answering Papa's phone?

'Is everything OK, Mum? Where's Papa?'

'Oh, nothing. It's no fuss. Everything is fine.'

'Mum,' I ask, flopping into Papa's chair. 'What's happening?'

She tells me that Papa wasn't feeling well, and his heart felt like it had been placed in an oven. He didn't want to make a fuss but they took him in to A&E.

'He had a minor heart attack. Very minor . . .'

'No fuss,' Papa groans in the background.

'We will be home tomorrow. He is fine. They just want to keep him in for observations. The doctor here is a good Gujarati. Remember Sanju's boy, Vimal? He calls it "obvs". So funny.'

I don't know what to say or how to react so I say nothing. Mum keeps asking if I'm still there until she hangs up and tries me again. I leave my phone on Papa's chair and go and sit on my bed, stunned.

23

When Mum and Papa return late the next morning, they come back to a changed household with a possessed Madhu.

Mate, I have spent an obscene amount of money on the old oat milk, on sweetener, on fruit and vegetables, on vitamin pills, on trainers for Papa. I am going to fix him.

They enter the main door downstairs just as I am sitting at the kitchen table, a bowl of freshly cut fruit in front of me, three empty bowls waiting for their fill, my fingers failing to type the right letters in a text and email and WhatsApp message and Instagram DM to Meena about Papa's heart attack. She needs to know. She doesn't need to feel like this puts reconciliation on her shoulders. But I feel like she needs to know.

I cannot for the life of me figure out how to write any of that without sounding like a sister who let her down.

I have lost my ability to communicate. I haven't spoken to anyone since Mum's phone call last night. I didn't even communicate with the guy at the shop who tried to engage me in chat.

I am voiceless.

When I hear the key in the lock of our front door, I fling my phone down on the table guiltily, like my mum has developed the ability to see screens through walls. I stand up and start piling fruit into bowls. I hear a shuffle in the doorway and turn around to see my father, wearing his big coat, which somehow makes him look smaller than he is. I hug him.

'It's OK, beti, all fine. No fuss. What is all of this?'

Wordlessly, I slip an arm around his waist and lead him to sit down. I place a bowl in front of him and pick my phone up from the table.

Mum enters.

'What's this? Fresh fruit? It's like we're staying in a hotel. Let me tell you, the best fruit salad I ever had was in Bombay.'

'Definitely,' Papa says. 'That hotel in Juhu where we stayed.'

'Papaya and mango and pineapple. Not all this katoo katoo rubbish we have in this country.'

Papa eats some fruit and carries on reminiscing about his trip with Mum to Bombay ten years ago, the only holiday they had taken in their entire lives together. It was for a wedding, so I don't even think it counts as a holiday. It still involved an obligation.

'Thank you for this, lovely,' Mum says, grabbing another bowl and sitting down to eat it.

'You're welcome,' I croak.

'This must have been expensive. Did you go to Ahsan's shop?'

I nod.

'Good, he is cheaper and his fruit must be eaten on the day.'

'He is so annoying,' Papa says. 'Always talking about how much he hates the British. I ask him once, "Why are you living here?" Know what he replied? He said, "You love the Indian cricket team and yet all I hear is you criticising the Indian cricket team. Pretend I am you and this awful country is the Indian cricket team." So annoying!'

Juice spills down Papa's chin. This is it. I cannot bring myself to ask him for details or find out how close he was to death. I miss being by myself, suddenly. I need to be in my room, watching something mindless on my laptop. Nothing funny. Only serious dramas for me. I consider *The Good Wife* or *The Good Fight*. Something involving the law. Something that shows me a wildly unrealistic but fun representation of what possibilities lie ahead for me as a lawyer.

The new life. The new life in the good fight.

As I walk to my bedroom, I text Meena:

Papa had a heart attack.

It's the most I can muster right now.

She replies, almost immediately:

I know. He texted me last night that he wants to see me. I'm on the train. See you shortly. You and I should talk at some point.

I lie on my bed and stare at the ceiling. I lose myself in the contours of paint on the Artex bumps.

I didn't buy the fruit from Ahsan's. I bought it from an overly expensive supermarket. Ahsan's selection was small and on the 'going off' side and I wanted it to feel like they were having breakfast in Bombay. The fruit bowls they had – there's a picture of them, framed, in our bathroom of all places. I see it every time I go to the toilet, and I think, *I wish I loved something, anything, as much as my mum loved those fruit bowls.*

I can tell it's Meena from the way she puts her key in the door. The familiar drop and jangle of her keyrings, charms and keys smashing together. It could only be her. She also always sighs in the same way over how her key for the top lock gets stuck and you have to pull it out and reinsert it till it's right. I bolt upright and spring off the bed. She's home!

Mood shifts, clouds part, the cracks in the sky let the light in, other beautiful descriptors to sum up how the adrenaline and dopamine rush through my entire body and trick me into thinking that I'm happy. I run out of my room and to the door to receive her.

I fix a smile on my face as I emerge from my bedroom and nearly barge into my sister.

'What's wrong? Why are you smiling weird?' Meena says.

She looks serious, dressed in that same Adidas tracksuit she used to wear on long journeys. Black, with the three stripes framing her edges. Her hair is escaping a ponytail arranged days ago. Her hands are covered by the ragged sleeves of the tracksuit, which feels old enough to be the middle sibling between me and my sister. I hold my arms out for a hug and she smiles and manages to squeeze past me in the tight entrance, into the flat, dropping her bag on to the floor and slipping off her chappals.

'Where's Kavita?' I ask.

'Where's Papa?' Meena asks, clearly enough so I know that this is not the best time to ask.

I close the door slowly, because I can feel my arms willing me to slam it in a counter strike to the grenade she just threw at me. I watch her disappear into the flat like she never left. She is immediately comfortable and part of me realises that she looks like she never left, because she didn't really leave. Her spirit has haunted these walls all this time.

I follow her and watch her stop in the entrance to the lounge, where Mum and Papa sleep. I quicken my step to follow, but she closes the door behind her. I stand there, waiting for her to open it and say, 'Jokes, babes, jokes', or something.

My phone vibrates.

It's a text from Danny.

Bus late?

Oh god, I have a shift.

24

My shift goes a bit better than the previous one. I create the character of the most charming possible waiter I can. And I serve those tables as Mads; she's working weekends and weeknights to put herself through university so she can become a defence lawyer and get her brother out of jail. She was definitely not an hour late for her shift. No way. Mads would never do that.

I serve pizzas, I serve drinks, I collect dirty plates, I smile through the terse banter of the chefs – an abrasive camaraderie I find jarring every shift – like I'm experiencing it for the first time.

Everything is going swimmingly until Jazz is seated in my station.

I don't notice till I hand the menus over and ask if he would like anything to drink. I focus on him and I realise. Oh god.

'Hey,' I say.

'Do you two know each other?' I hear in the poshest, driest, most nasal, yaaaa-yaaaa voice I have ever heard in my life. That's when the perfume worms its way up my nostrils and takes root inside my sinuses for ever. I am never going to smell anything again. A newborn baby's head, freshly cut grass, freshly cut mango, my own farts, which are secretly delicious in their offensiveness.

I turn to the voice and see the poshest woman ever. She is brown royalty or something. Probably has paintings of Mughals all over her house. She has gold rings on every finger, gold exploding from her nose, gold hanging off her ears, even gold in a haircut that performs no functional duties; it's too gold for that.

She looks like she's walked off the set of one of those Hindi dramas where thirty-seven out of forty minutes are in slow motion.

'This is my mum,' Jazz says, clearing his throat, ruffling the back of his neck, grimacing. Three classic stressed-Jazz moves.

'Hey, Jazz's mum,' I say.

'Hello, dear,' Jazz's mum says. 'My name is Jasminder.'

'So you're a Jazz too. Hilarious,' I say, laughing into the silence that follows.

'Are you sure this is a good place?' Jasminder asks Jazz, like I have disappeared to get the chefs to prepare the caviar pizza and the golden platter it must be served on.

Jazz nods and looks up at me.

'And this is my friend, Madhu. She's a hilarious comedian.'

Jasminder rolls her eyes, like, *Oh how tedious, another funny clown*, and turns to her lap where she fiddles with the clasp of a handbag.

'You two are comedy friends? What a droll delight. And you work here?'

'Gotta pay them bills,' I say. 'Can I get you a drink?'

Jasminder looks up at me, as if she's stunned by the thought that I could be a comedian and have a job as well. Mind. Blown. For. Some. Reason. Who. Are. These. People?

I fetch them their drinks order and hover around the other tables, doing my jokes, looking between Jazz, who keeps staring at me, and the clock on the wall between the kitchen and the main restaurant, which tells me how much longer I have on my shift. I want to be home and in my family's space. And not here.

I'm summoned to a table where a couple sits.

'Everything OK?' I ask, beaming, sensing these types aren't tippers but they haven't given me a reason to dial back the charm. They look like a young married couple on their first date night in months. He wears his only shirt without baby juice on it and she has really dressed up, squeezed into a nostalgia-inducing dress to try and make herself feel like it's not all that bad really.

'Settle an argument for us,' he says, looking over at his wife, who stifles a laugh. 'The word dungarees is Indian, right?'

I fold my arms, sighing. Another night, another call-up to be the expert on all things Indian for white people. Honestly, it's a sickness. I've been asked about yoga poses, to recommend the best Indian spot in the city (you know, the one where all you lot go cos it's so authentic), about the percentage of Muslim people living in the country, about the prime minister's incredibly fascist politics, and now about whether dungarees are, like the *Goodness Gracious Me* sketch probably told us, Indian. Oh Lord Bhagwan, give this atheist strength.

'Why are you asking me?'

'Because,' the guy says, slowly looking up at me and making eye contact. I can see the panic in his tiny guinea-pig eyes. 'I just assumed you would know.'

'Why?' I ask again. 'Why me?'

'He didn't mean any . . .' his partner says, meekly, like she's recoiling from the abject aggression of my words.

'I just assumed . . .'

'You know what my mum used to say . . .?' I say. She didn't say this phrase. I just don't want to attribute it to myself. I want them to know this is the kind of smarmy crap you say to children. 'When you assume, you make an ASS out of U and ME. See what I'm saying, right?'

'See? I think dungarees are definitely American. They're slave costumes, surely,' the wife says and I put on my smile, feeling Jazz's eyes bore into me from across the room.

'Can I get you anything else?' I say. 'I'm not allowed to mediate in disagreements between customers unless it turns violent, in which case I will act. However, it goes against the pizza-waiter code to engage in the debate. No matter how racist.'

'Come on,' the guy says. 'It's one of those other words, like gymkhana and pyjama and bandana and cashmere, right? Indian words we stole, right?'

'Come on, dude, I'm trying to work. I'm not a walking encyclopaedia of India, just cos I'm brown. I don't ask you white-guy shit like why Kanye is actually a proper artiste, or why *Mad Men*'s sexism and racism is actually cool, or why railways were a good exchange for all the resource- and asset-stripping the British Empire did. Right? You can't just go around assuming people like me will drop everything to answer your facile questions that you've decided we must know the answers to because of the colour of our skin. I would tell you what word we use to describe that behaviour but I'm actually just wondering, seeing as it's my job to do so, that your wine is looking a little low. Would you like another bottle?'

I've attracted some attention. Oh god. I've done it. Oops, I did it again; shouts to Britney Spears. People applaud. Jazz, leading the charge. His mum applauds me too, looking at me with new eyes. Danny is hovering.

The man looks at Danny.

'Hi, is there a problem? I'm the manager . . .' Danny says, looking at me, standing close to me, his hand on my back, holding me up.

'Yes, I'm afraid so, this is outrageous. Your waiter just called me a racist.'

'Your wine is looking a little low,' Danny says. 'Can I get you any more?'

The man shakes his head.

'Is that all you have to say?' his partner says, in that whiny voice that people have when they're defending their mates' awful behaviour. You really get an insight into who they were at school and what type of school it was. In my school, you'd get sparked for that kind of voice. In hers, she wouldn't, cos her dad's a Lord or something.

'Look,' Danny says. 'I trust my staff in all matters. I didn't hear her call you a racist. If anything, I thought she was being generous to you. She's right, her only job here is to ensure your food and drink needs are met. She is not the arbiter of all things you assume her culture to be because of the colour of her skin. And she doesn't need rescuing, so I'm going to step out. Madhu, you're brilliant.'

Danny backs away and starts collecting plates from another table in my station where the diners have finished but I haven't got to yet, because of these fools.

'Wine?' I ask.

'The bill, please,' the man says. 'We're done. Don't expect a tip.'

'I could tell the second I seated you, don't worry, darling,' I say, smiling as I walk away with their plates.

Jazz gestures to talk to me on my way past him, but I shrug away his hand.

'I'm working, man. Stop being weird. And stop showing up at my work to have a chat. Text me like a normal person,' I hiss.

'I'm sorry for abandoning you,' he whispers.

'That's a start,' I whisper back.

* * *

199

When my shift finishes and Danny has commended me on my ability to deal with difficult customers, I head out on to the street. I'm anxious to get home and stomp to the bus. I hear a beep and someone shouting my name. Next to the bus stop, I see Jazz, in a car that could only belong to a parent, engine on, window down, leaning out.

'Want a lift?'

I approach the car and crouch down to see who else is with him.

'Where's your mum?' I ask.

'Oh, she's gone to Temple Meads. Weekend in London with friends. I just dropped her.'

'Great, sure,' I say, and get into the passenger side of the car.

It's immaculately clean inside. Like it's brand new but nostalgic for a few decades ago in its upholstery. It smells of car freshener and the type of aftershave a teenage boy gets gifted by a well-meeting aunt who doesn't know them well for Christmas. Jazz smiles at me as I drop into my seat and fiddle around for a seatbelt. I give him my address and he punches it into his satnav.

'The apology road,' I say. 'I guess it has two lanes.'

'You don't have to . . .'

'I got carried away. Worst of all, I got carried away by the wrong crowd. Can you believe that?'

'What on earth did I watch?' Jazz says, smiling and pulling out on to the road, cautiously.

'Kareena was super nice to me, to make me all vulnerable.

Then she brought on Marvin to turn the tables on me so the audience would laugh at me thinking I was being brought on as a hero but actually I was being brought on as the villain. And then she lectured me about teaching me a lesson about comedy, and how it's a hard road and if I can't rise to the challenge, then I have no business in the business. Since then, you know, my life has fallen apart. My sister hates me even more for spilling the family secrets on national television, Papa had a minor heart attack – he's fine by the way – oh and to top it all off, I seem to have become bad at waitressing, which I thought I was good at. I have lost my voice, I never want to do comedy again, I'll become a lawyer, at which university I don't know, and I'm just sitting here monologuing in your car, when actually all I need to say is, sorry for being an idiot to you.'

'Wow, that is a lot. And there I was, needing to find a way to apologise to you for leaving you cos I was jealous. You seemed so at ease, like this was your world, not mine. And I've decided to also give up comedy and pick a career. All signs point to some kind of business thing so I can go work with my dad in Dubai. Fun Times McGee, look at us.'

'We coulda been the best, you and me,' I say, in some sort of New York socialite voice. 'We coulda been stars.'

'I think Kareena would have murdered us. She's very much the unicorn brown, right?'

'What's a unicorn brown?' I ask.

'My mum said it, when I spoke to her about the whole thing. She said there are different kinds of browns in this world, whatever industry you find yourself in. There are unicorn browns, who are usually the only brown person in the room and they feel uncomfortable when another brown arrives. They welcome you but they gaslight you without ever really understanding or realising they're doing it. Cos they're professionally threatened. And then there's the elite browns, the establishment browns, who are in the position they're in cos of money and power and they hold that power and they hate all the inclusion chat cos they're like, my daddy's money got me here on my own merit so why is everyone complaining. And they usually say stuff like, I'm not interested in any conversation about race unless we speak about class. And what they mean is, the upper classes. They have no interest in working-class politics. And so you go, OK cool, let's talk about class, and you never hear from them again. Anyway, look at me, monologuing my mum's pet theories.'

'Your mum sounds cool,' I say, feeling guilty over the assumptions I made about her. 'I didn't realise she knew you were trying stand-up.'

'Oh, yeah. She knows all about it. She knows it's a thing I wanna do and she always assumed it was a hobby.' He pauses, turning on to my road. 'I let her think that. But the sad thing is, she was right and I wasn't.'

'You're good, Jazz. Really good.'

'Nah, you were right. I'm too stiff. I can't improvise. I have to know my material and stick to it. There's no real science to stand-up that fully omits instinct.'

'True, true,' I say. 'What does it really even matter, anyway?'

'You have such a distinct voice though,' Jazz says.

He pulls up outside our block and I sit there, my legs weak; I feel heavy and unable to move.

'Did I? I think that was Kareena's point. I have nothing to say.'

'Of course you do, you just haven't fully worked it out yet. You're seventeen. You have time!'

'And so life goes,' I reply, murmuring slightly, angling my body away from him as I open the door and extract myself from the car. 'Listen, Jazz, you're a good guy. Thank you for brokering the peace deal. I appreciate it. I have so many people mad at me right now, I was bewildered about where to start. That was classy of you. Thank you, bro.'

'What can I say?' Jazz says. 'Weirdly, I missed you. Who else in my life is around to make me feel so horrible about myself?'

'Your dad?'

'Only in person. When he's in Dubai, it's all cricket and updates on my studies over text.'

'Let's hang out soon,' I say. 'Like, properly. Not like a vague thing you might say to an acquaintance. I mean it, pals, hang-outs, doing stuff. I've never walked across the suspension bridge. Let's do that.'

'Let's do that,' Jazz says, laughing at me. 'What about now?'

I look back towards my block, feeling the pull of my family. I shake my head and wave goodbye, turning to face home. Anxious to see my sister, my dad better, all of it, I run over to the front door. Jazz beeps as he pulls away, I stop to wave at him before fumbling in my bag for my keys.

I get so frustrated that my fingers don't find them easily so I crouch down and empty my bag on the floor. Just to add drama to the urgency of it all, a thorough rain shower decides to mess with me, drenching everything. I rescue my phone first, because I'm no fool, then my wallet, then all the ChapSticks I keep buying, only to find the ones lost in the vortex of this bag. Then I realise I didn't even bring my keys with me because I was in such a rush.

I press the buzzer for our flat.

I hear interference and then my sister's voice. It sounds so much like home I could cry.

'Hello?' she asks, rude and confused like always.

'It's me, I forgot my keys.'

'Who is this?' she asks curtly.

Our little routine. It's back. My heart is singing and aching.

'Oh hey,' I say, doing the bit. 'I'm just an assassin. Your roof looks cool, can I come in and check it out? It's definitely not so I can use it for one of my assassinations.'

I hear the buzzer go and the door is released. No words from her, no laugh or chuckle or comeback. Just the *whaaaaarrrr* sound unlocking the door. I open it, realising she's not ready yet. Not yet. But she might be with time.

Inside the building, I bound up the stairs, hearing the flat's door open above. I expect to see Meena in the doorway tutting, arms folded, a faux-lecture about responsibility, maybe even twirling my keys on her little finger for emphasis.

No one.

I enter the flat and it smells of chai and Mum's cooking. I hear murmurs coming from the kitchen and I rush in, expecting everyone to welcome me home. It's amazing. Having them all home. It's perfect. Really makes me realise what I have been missing all this time. How utterly bereft of a family experience I've been.

Happy families. Just utter happy families. It's what I've been yearning for.

I walk into the kitchen. Papa is sitting at the table, drinking tea. Mum is at the hob, turning theplas. Meena is nowhere to be seen.

'Where's Meena?' I say, urgently, a pang of separation anxiety acidic in the depths of my stomach.

'She's in her room. We need to have a conversation,' Papa says. 'Please sit down, Madhu.'

'Oh, OK, everything OK?' I ask, sitting down.

'We need to talk about Kareena Patel.'

Oh. Oh no.

25

The only time my father has had to discipline me is when I broke a toilet. It's my fault, Your Honour, but cause and effect are important things to establish. I put it to you that during a long, hot summer where two siblings are suddenly old enough to stay in their house and do school work instead of going to the shop, but it's only on pain of death that they're allowed to leave the flat, they're both still young . . . well, I put it to you that in that scenario, in that stuffy flat, they're going to run around the place with water pistols they got in party bags like ten years ago.

There's me and Meena, screaming and running. Spraying each other. Nowhere on our bodies is safe. The carpet is getting increasingly sopping. And we don't care. We are laughing and laughing at this fake freedom we've been given. The run of the house. Everything is up for grabs.

When I go for a refill in the bathroom, the tap water, full throttle, hits the water pistol and bounces up and on to the walls around me. Meena, in the bath with the shower curtain around her, waiting for her own reload safe zone, laughs at me. I realise this is probably too much now. Because water has gone all over Mum and Papa's wedding photo, which is, for some reason, mounted by the toilet. Maybe so Papa can stare at it while he does his business.

Anyway, guiltily, I worry about water finding its way behind the plastic of the frame, so I grab a towel and wipe it down. I'm in a rush, which makes me clumsy, and as I wipe the frame, it falls off its nail and a corner smashes the top of the toilet cistern, shattering it in half, as the picture frame explodes everywhere.

It's a million to one shot that shatters the top of the toilet. Meena laughs and then stops when she sees that half of the cistern lid is now missing. I stare at it, frozen, unsure of what even to do in the situation. I stare at it like I need my big sister to take over and work out how to salvage this mess. All she does is push past me and fish out the photo of Mum and Papa floating in the water of the cistern.

The way Papa tells us both off, he is attempting to be furious but you can also tell he finds this funnier than he should. He shouts and then expresses pride that as sisters we formed a unit and didn't try to throw each other under the bus. In the end he hugs us.

To this day, the toilet has not been fixed. But a new wedding photo watches over it.

I think of the peculiar way he told us off that day, and the callous way he threw Meena out, not raising his voice once, mostly clinical, mostly a Liam Neeson film, mostly cold and methodical in his removal of her.

'I saw your Kareena Patel performance,' Papa tells me. 'It was on Channel 4 repeats when I was in the hospital and I could not sleep. I have a question for you . . .'

I want to die, I want to run, I want to fall down at my father's feet and beg forgiveness. Like some big, dramatic Bollywood film, a big string crescendo telling the world that it is all my fault.

'What's that?' I croak, as all the moisture in my throat decides now is the time to retreat into my glands, or wherever moisture goes – I'm no biologist, I'm a lawyer, Your Honour. I only care about the law.

'Why were you so shy? This was your big opportunity. You have been talking about being on television and doing comedy for so long. And you get to be on that person's show? And you bottle it? Beti, what happened?'

I don't understand. Why isn't my father mad at me? For lying about where I was, about airing family secrets on television, for being embarrassing. Why is he being all 'what we did well, what we could have done better' like my teachers do in post-exam analysis. I'm so confused.

'Aren't you mad?'

'Yes,' he says. 'Not at you. Not any more.'

Mum puts plates between us, thepla for her and me, with a side of chundo. For Papa, a stick of celery, with chundo. Small steps, I guess.

'Beti, ever since you were born, this is what you wanted to do,' Mum tells me. The way she speaks about my life and the things I've said, it's like she means another person.

'Tell jokes? That's not true,' I say.

'Perform. You were always performing, dancing, telling stories, acting out things, and when we would notice, you would always get so shy . . .'

'I never understood, beti. You always wanted our attention and then when you got it, you didn't know what to do with it.'

This makes some sense to me. This idea of wanting to tell the world I had something to say and then when the world stopped for me, realising I had nothing. Like, I'm happy to talk back in class or pile on or make fun. But if the teacher asks me for my opinion or an answer, I freeze. It's strange. I never thought that was a thing. I just thought it's cos I didn't care about school.

'Darling, why did you go on that show?'

'Because . . .' I stammer. 'I thought Kareena could help me with my comedy career. I thought then maybe I wouldn't have to do the law thing. Cos law seems so boring, innit.'

'Darling, you can do whatever you want. I just want you to have a foundation in something,' Papa says. 'I don't like it when parents put all their expectations for their lives on to their children.'

Who is this man and what has he done with my father? I feel like one of those cartoon rodents whose jaw has just fallen to the floor.

'I always wanted to go to university,' Mum says. 'I made Papa promise me. When we have a bit more money and we are settled, I want to do something. I always loved English. I thought I could do that.'

'What happened?' I ask, welling up despite me bulging out my eyes as wide as possible to try and stop the tears.

'We had the shop and then Meena and then you, and then I was in my fifties and thought, I don't have time any more.'

'I always wanted your mum to go. It was the only thing she asked. And I failed her.'

'You didn't fail me,' Mum says.

'Listen,' Papa tells me. 'The university thing, I realised recently, is me putting on to you and Meena my expectations for life. I should have listened to what you wanted. Life is too short to not follow your dreams and life is too short to fight with the ones you love. I don't know best for your life. Only you do. If you want to be a comedian, do that.'

'But better than you did on Kareena's show . . .' Mum adds.

'You're not angry with me?' I ask, confused.

'I was,' Papa says. 'But you know what Mum said to me?' I shake my head. 'Why did our daughter hide this from us?'

'It's true,' Mum says, getting up and adding a second thepla to my plate, covering up the uneaten one already there.

'It was your big night and you hid it from us.'

'Papa, I thought you'd think it was stupid.'

'What I saw *was* stupid. You are better than that. If anything, I was annoyed you didn't get to do better.'

'Me too,' I tell him, tearing the thepla and dipping it in the chundo. 'I'm angry about what Kareena did to me. We were

210

talking before and she was being all big sister to me and asked me all these questions and I guess, you know, whatever anyone thinks about what happened with my sister, it's been on my mind ever since she left, like, it affects my every thought, my every action, and I just spilled. And then Kareena used it to make me feel bad on television. And then I left, and I feel bad cos now everyone knows our business. I've said sorry to Meena.'

'She said,' Mum says. 'She says you came to see her.'

Papa reaches across the table for my hand. I keep it hovering over my plate. I'm still holding on to an uneaten, gloopy torn-off bit of thepla. I don't feel like I want this to be easy for him. I'm happy he hasn't told me off for going on television. That took the wind out of my sails a bit. But that's just the beginning.

'I don't want your apology,' he says.

'I'm not giving you one,' I tell him.

'Oh, darling,' Mum says. 'I think it was exactly what your papa needed. What we both needed. We needed to be embarrassed by what we had done. To someone in our family. One of us.'

'I want to . . .' Papa says, then pauses, looking out of the window, because . . . my dad starts crying. He is crying. He is crying actual sad tears of emotion. I don't know what to do with myself. I have literally never heard him cry. He didn't cry when Mum shut his hand in the bedroom door; when Ba died; when Dumbo's mum is chained up at the circus and they curl trunks around each other; or in the moments after

211

Meena left, looking him in the eye and saying, 'I cannot believe you are doing this to me.'

But now, the looking out of the window and trying to hold tears back is just enough of a spurt of crying momentum to open the levees and let the tears flood the kitchen.

He places the tips of his thumb and index fingers into his eye sockets and pushes hard – like that's going to stop him.

I sit frozen the entire time. A wail comes then stops; he holds up a hand as if to say, one second, I'll be fine, then he says, 'I need to say thank you.'

He opens his eyes and looks at me, his lips shaking, his eyes drooping, the gravity of sadness pulling them towards the table.

'Go on then,' I say, and Mum glares at me, like I'm being heartless or something. But I know what I'm doing.

It cuts the tension enough for him to clasp his hands together and bring them down like a hammer on to the table, making us all jump with the jangle of cutlery and mugs across the surface.

'What?' he says.

'I'm not letting you get off that easily, Papa. Things have not been good in our family for a while. And I cannot be silent about it any longer. I will not continue to play the dutiful daughter just because you are happy with how I live my life. I still hid it from you. All these years. Ask yourself why?'

'Madhu, beti . . .' he says, but I hold up my hand.

Before I can really think about what I'm saying, I feel the surge of power from the heavens reach me and I speak, I just speak. It's time for me to speak.

'I'm going to let you finish, Papa, because you don't owe me a thanks. You owe me a sorry. You owe me a sorry for putting me in the middle of you and my sister. You owe me a sorry for putting pressure on me to do what you think is best without ever asking me what I think is best. You owe me a sorry for putting me in a position where I hide the most important thing about myself. I love comedy. I love laughing. I love making people laugh. I love being a comedian. You owe me a sorry for making the light of the world a bit dimmer when you threw my sister out, told me to never contact her or I'd be out of here too and to go to university like I've been told. Also, you owe me a sorry for borrowing my travel mug and leaving it in the shop and me finding it, six months later, with black mould all over it in the stock room. You said you gave it back, made me feel irresponsible for losing it and then made me pay twelve pounds, twelve pounds I don't have easily to hand, to buy a new one. When it was you. So either you say sorry for making yourself into the infallible father who is never wrong, or say thank you to me for making the biggest humiliation of my life also the biggest humiliation of yours, or just bring my sister home.'

My father stands up and leaves the room. I look at Mum and she gets up from the table, shaking her head, busying herself with getting spices out for cooking.

I sit there, holding my hands the way Papa did, and I realise, I'm not even annoyed for letting my voice get me into trouble. If anything, I did the right thing by telling the truth for a second.

I feel liberated.

Papa comes back into the room with a stack of things in his hand. He drops some papers in front of me.

'What's this?' I say but then I notice my handwriting. I leaf through the papers.

Oh god, I can't believe he kept them. I had completely forgotten about these. When I was around eleven, Papa would wear the same coat to work, whether it was burning hot or freezing cold, and I would slip a joke into his pocket. It'd be a silly observation like, 'Cows have never been to the moon and humans can't make cheese, why?' or a joke, like a little in-joke that only made sense to us. My favourite, I read now, is 'Why did the pea fall on its head? It wasn't. It was a carrot.' I don't even know why this was funny at the time, but I remember it made us laugh and laugh and laugh. So I wrote it down and recorded it for ever.

After the first joke, he came home chuckling and told me how funny and sweet it was and, buoyed by this, I wrote him another, and another, and another. I kept this up for a good while, I don't know – maybe six months, and then after a week visiting family in Leicester with Mum and Meena, I stopped. Maybe after hanging out for a week with cousins a lot older than me, I had a better yardstick for what was cool and what was age-appropriate, or I broke the habit, or I had a self-conscious voice in my head. Whatever it was, it stopped this little transaction between me and Papa dead.

'I can't believe you kept these,' I say.

'Why? If I want anyone to know anything about my daughter,

I tell them about this. I tell them she is the funniest person I have ever met.'

'What's your point, Papa?'

'You think you know what I think of you? Sure, I have pushed you towards some security. That is what any good parent should do. But I have never ever told you what to do. You told me you should do law . . . not me.'

'Papa, just because you didn't say the words, it doesn't mean that the intention didn't put pressure on me.'

Papa stops and looks at me, he stands up tall and he strokes at my neck. I hunch forward to release myself from this intrusion, my fingers amongst the relics of my past comedy career.

'I'm sorry, I didn't realise that was what I was doing.'

'You made me feel like I had no choice,' I tell him. Now *I* want to cry. So much for the victory moment.

'You can do anything you want,' Papa tells me. 'I think you would make a fine comedian. This is what you made me realise. When I saw you on that show, you were not you. Kareena Patel had turned you into what she wanted you to be. I wanted to see you, I wanted to hear you. And I realised. My daughter is doubting she is funny. Baby, baby girl, you can be whoever you want to.'

OK, yeah, fine, now I'm crying, ladies and gentlemen. Now I'm crying.

26

We're waiting for Meena to come home. She said she was popping out to get some stuff now she was back in Bristol. I don't imagine we'll see her till late. She'll have friends to talk to about her life and stuff.

Papa and I watch television, a stand-up special I've chosen. An old Josie Long one that fills me with hopes and good feelings. She has a joke about how if you want something beautiful to exist you have to make it for yourself.

Papa hands me something he has been clutching and shielding since he emerged with the stack of my notes. The special has ended and we've been sitting in silence since. Mum has volunteered to go to the shop to give us time to reconnect.

'What is this?' I ask, taking the photo and holding it up to the light.

'It's a picture of me,' Papa says.

Sure enough, there's Papa, with a guitar, sitting on a wall overlooking the sea, with another guy tapping away on a small drum.

'Would you believe . . . ?' Papa says. 'I found this guitar.

Someone was throwing it out and I climbed into a skip and got it. Luckily, one of my teachers at school used to play and he helped me restring it and he taught me some chords for some Beatles songs. And me and my friend Sunil, we used to go to sit and look out over the sea and play. No one would give us any money but we laughed and laughed and made up songs and had a brilliant time. It made me so happy to make him happy, to sing these funny songs about people walking past.' Papa is wearing a cool 70s shirt, colourful, very red, big collar to match the big sideburns, his hair like a bird's wing flapping in the wind, his gamcha tied round him like a dhoti, barefoot, overlooking the sunset at Worle beach.

'What are you trying to show me, Papa?' I say, laughing. 'Oh, Madhu beti, I too was a goofy artist with broken dreams?'

'No,' Papa says, laughing. 'I wanted to show you that I could have been an artist too. I'm not closed to the idea.'

'No, this is you saying, look at what I sacrificed for you kids to be here. I could be sitting on a wall at Worle beach, playing guitar with my buddy right now. I did this all for you. It's a subtle-pressure reminder, Pops. I know what you're doing.'

'That's not true, Madhu. Why won't you ever listen to what's being said? You always decide how people feel. You never trust us enough to tell you anything.'

His voice has risen. He looks upset.

'Who does that remind you of, Papa?' I say, calmly.

'Exactly,' my father says, hugging me. 'And look at all the mistakes I made. No more.'

I understand what he's saying. I'm hearing it. I hug him back.

'Maybe all that jumping to conclusions about everyone is what gave me a heart attack,' Papa says and laughs, doubling over until I join him.

Later, Papa asks me if I want him to message Kareena's producers and tell them to get her to apologise, and I laugh and say no. Because I'm not having my pops bail me out. He even says he could sue them for having an under-eighteen on the show without a chaperone. Again, I decline.

'If only you knew a lawyer,' I say and he laughs.

When Meena comes home she walks up to the sofa and hugs me from behind and asks what's going on and with her arms around me, the way they used to be, my mouth goes warm and dry and I forget to speak. I just bask in her softness, in the fetid sweat smell of her unwashed T-shirt. I don't care. I could bathe in it for ever.

And then I forget about Kareena Patel and revenge, because Meena asks if we want to meet someone.

I stand up and watch as Saeed and Mum walk into the room. Mum is beaming and holding aloft a niece like she is showing the cub successor the savannah over which it will one day rule: my Kavita. Dressed all in white – poor choice for a baby that voms and poops a lot. The baby is a chonk, two dollops of ice cream, a smiling, gurning solid unit, the type of bulging, healthy thighs you could bite into. I shriek and hold my arms out. Kavita stares at me, unsure of what to make of me – then slams her head backwards into Mum and looks around, panicking. Spotting Meena, she holds her hands out.

Mum clutches her tighter.

'If she needs you every time she's upset,' Mum says assertively over the squawks, 'then you are the only one who can comfort her.'

'Mum,' Meena says. 'I'm not going to force her to be with anyone she doesn't want to be with, OK? That's abusive.'

'She wants to be with me,' Mum says. 'She just saw your sister and freaked out.'

Meena laughs and takes Kavita from Mum, sitting down on the sofa, crossing her legs under her and making faces at Kavita who immediately giggles, the fickle idiot.

I ask Saeed, standing awkwardly, hands in front of him, if he wants a tea. He shakes his head and says he's taking his mum to mosque in a second. I give him a hug because it's so weird to see him as part of the fabric of our family instead of the secret boyfriend creeping about, sneaking out, locking eyes with me to ensure I hold the secrets too. And now, here he is. All the secrets were leading to this: him announcing he's taking his mum to mosque like he's been one of our family the entire time. I love it.

I can tell he's unsure about the cuddle, not from how tightly his arms grip me, but how he curls his top half backwards, like he's trying to escape. I release him and turn my attention to the baby.

I jump around, one-eighty degrees like a gangster, and I fall to my knees pointing at Kavita, who stares at me, gnawing at a plastic watermelon.

'Listen, baby. I am going to make you love me, OK? I don't mean this in a creepy way. But I am your masi, you hear me? Madhu masi is going to make you love her. You are going to find me hilarious and real, I will probably be the one to buy you your first cocktail. I don't even like cocktails. Here's a tumbler of sugar water – pay me forty pounds, please? No thank you. I will introduce you to the cuisines of the world, and the best comedians, and the books that are so good that in the years to come, when they get turned into a television show, we get to be all smug that we read the source material years ago. I am going to be your Marvel Cinematic Universe buddy. And your snuggle buddy. And I will read to you whenever you want and then when I am old and living in the granny flat at the end of your two-acre garden, you can read to me, because life is a circle. OK, little lady. So you be all stoosh now, that's fine. But it won't last for ever. And when you're mine, you will be mine. Best buds for ever. I will love you more than my own kids too. Mostly because I have no interest in having kids so this is a sci-fi thought experiment at best. So, you know what? Take all the time you need, kid. Because you know what I also have? Time . . .'

I bow to Kavita, who carries on staring at me like she's nervous of me, and I stand and bow to my audience. Mum is beaming, Papa is holding on to the back of the sofa, crying with laughter, and even Saeed, the stony-faced assassin, has smirked.

I'm back, baby. Ladies and gentlemen, I'm back.

* * *

I float through the rest of the evening like a frog on a lily pad without a care in the world or a frog with it in their sights. I laugh and laugh as we play with Kavita and she slowly warms to me. I start to learn that to babies, neediness from adults is as unattractive as I find it to be, as a nearly adult. We eat a feast. Mum makes all Meena's favourites and Papa holds Meena's hand like he will never let go and Kavita tussles for her mum's attention back.

When Saeed returns a few hours later, Mum goes on about what a good boy he is and moans about how we have never taken her to the mandhir and we all laugh about how she is so unreligious she doesn't even keep a mandap in the house, and Papa keeps saying how much he has missed this. Time passes quickly, because it is passing as it should and not like it's imbued with longing. None of us in that room want for anything other than to be in that room in that moment and for however long it lasts is how long we need it.

When it's just me and Meena, watching television, cuddled up on the sofa – well, me cuddled into her, oblivious to any space issues she might have – Kareena Patel's show comes on and I reach for the remote control and turn it off.

'I'm outraged she made you doubt yourself,' Meena says.

I sit up and force myself on to the edge of the sofa.

'It's probably for the best,' I say. 'I doubt I would have gone anywhere with it.'

Meena laughs and leans forward, picking up what must be a

lukewarm mug of peppermint tea, because sipping between points always gives you the upper hand. Such a power move.

'With respect . . .' Meena says, then hesitates, because she's about to deliver a death stroke, 'you're seventeen. How on earth do you know what's going anywhere? Your life has barely started. Don't close the world off just because it didn't go well once. Earlier, when you were monologuing at your niece, you came alive.'

Meena switches the television on. Kareena's face is now in my peripheral vision. Something about it undoes me.

'That's rich coming from you. You had a baby. Your life is over.'

'Not if I wanted a baby.' Meena sighs. A disappointed sigh. 'Bit mean of you to throw that at me. I am fine with my choices. I left because other people weren't. I never thought that was you. Ever.'

I stumble over my thoughts. I never thought I thought that until I said it. Am I disappointed in my sister for having a baby?

'I'm sorry,' I say. 'I don't think I meant that.'

'Either you think it, or you said it to hurt me, knowing it would hurt me, knowing you don't even believe it. Either way is horrible, sis. I thought better of you.'

Meena stands up and slurps her tea, that loud, obsessively dramatic noise she does to annoy me.

'I said it to hurt you,' I say, not even knowing the truth of it, but knowing this is the lesser of the offences.

'You really think you're funny, don't you?' she tells me, and I want to throw myself to the floor and hide for ever.

27

Look, I put that dramatic pause in there, ladies and gentlemen, because I'm not proud of what happened next. It involved me standing up and pushing my sister and her dropping her peppermint tea and me feeling guilty about the shove and the stain, which is luckily in the folds of her tracksuit.

I wipe at her silently with my own T-shirt and then I start trying to soak up the tea with the palms of my hands. The hoodie is warm, the bottoms are warm, her body is warm, she is my sister, I cannot believe the one person whose opinion trumps everyone else's thinks I'm not funny.

So my mopping up of the tea becomes more outrageous, more elaborate. I snake a hand under her hoodie to catch the tea from the inside.

And finally, she breaks, bursting out laughing.

'OK, OK, stop,' she says.

'Admit I'm funny.'

'Fine,' she says. 'You're immature and mean sometimes and I love you and you're funny, now get off me.'

She chuckles as she leaves the room. The whole interaction wasn't great. But. I'm funny.

That is what matters.

As I try to sleep that night, I keep thinking about why it matters to me that I'm funny. Like, why is that my thing?

In the dark, I hear the door open and someone slips into the room. From the way she sighs, constantly, I know it's my sister.

'Budge up,' she whispers. 'Saeed's got the baby so I need to sleep.'

'Oh, OK. Cos I'm very awake and I need to ask you something.'

A sigh. Then an 'OK,' and I smile as my sister cuddles into me, kicking the quilt off because of her hot feet. She is still wearing the tracksuit. It smells of baby sick and peppermint tea.

'What is my voice?'

'What do you mean?'

'Like, I'm thinking about what sort of comedy I like and I miss telling jokes, and I stupidly threw away all my notebooks. I'm not saying I'm about to head to Edinburgh. But, like, it's just good to know what my voice is. Kareena said I didn't have one and that's why she wanted to show me what that felt like.'

'The real question is,' Meena whispers, 'why do you care so much what Kareena Patel says and thinks? She's famous. Sure. She's your hero. Sure. But you're not equals. She'll never see you as one. You can't go from being someone's hero to seeing them as an equal. No matter how humble you think you are.'

'You think?' I say.

'Yeah, of course. The problem is, *you* think about what she thinks. And it matters to you. Of course. She's your hero. But you need to just work out what you want to say and do and do it loads, and if she rates you then, she rates you. If not, then fine. But it's on you to be the person, the comedian you want to be.'

'So what she was saying was right?'

'Yeah, she was just cruel. Like, that's not a very inspirational way to go about it. Like, she's supposed to give you space to grow. Not hold up a mirror to where you haven't.'

I turn around in the darkness so my sister is cuddling me. Her voice is getting slower and slurrier; she needs the sleep.

'Last question,' I say. 'How do I shove this in her face? How cruel she was.'

'The real question,' Meena says, slowly, quietly, fading into dreams, 'is why it matters to you to get revenge on her. Just do you.'

'Just do you' is the three-word mantra of the day for the next few days. I swap shifts so Mum and I can take Kavita to the park so Saeed and Meena can get more sleep.

Playing with Kavita is a joy and soon I have won her over and she giggles audibly at everything I do. I realise that I'm just doing me around her. I want to show her the joys of life. You know when you pull a silly face or contort your body into a weird spatial dance move that delights, and then someone demands you do it again. But actually, the moment has gone for ever and you existed so thoroughly in it for the briefest of moments, that for a second – just one tiny fragment of a segment – you were a gorgeous hilarious being.

That's what I experience.

And then my sister and my niece and my . . . Saeed head to the train station in a taxi. And I cry saying goodbye but we make plans for a few weekends for me to visit. And I don't mourn them going because actually this feels like the start of something.

I walk into college the next day with the just-do-you mindset and Shanai and Marvin invite me for a coffee and we don't mention the tensions, we just chat about uni stuff and I admit to them both I'm so conflicted about the whole endeavour, and Shanai says that I should just follow my heart like she did with the love of her life, and Marvin grabs her face and kisses her, before breaking away and saying, 'Look at London. That's where all the comedy stuff is.'

When a teacher comes over to talk to Shanai about an after-school debate she's running about cancel culture (lol big lol), it's just me and Marvin and I know the thing between us that's left unsaid is the Kareena of it all. I want to know and I don't. What was he doing? Why was she so terrible to me? I have Meena in my head telling me it doesn't matter what she thinks.

'I'm sorry about what went down,' he says. I look to him. He's leaning forward, elbows on knees, hands clasped, head bowed like he's getting a pep talk from coach.

'It's cool, we don't need to talk about it.'

'I mean,' Marvin says. 'What you said made me realise how

awful I'd been to Shanai. So I guess I have to thank you for making me confront how awful I was. Keeping speaking truth to power, I guess.'

'Oh, Marvin, are you in power now? Is that what you're saying? How mighty of you, to admit you're the man; a man tells me he is the man. Great . . .' I stop. 'Sorry, I'm doing it again.'

'It's funny,' Marvin says. 'It's uncomfortable.' He sighs, like he's thinking about it. 'It's uncomfortable for sure, but it's funny. Isn't that the best thing? That you make someone confront crappy stuff about themselves and then before they know it, they're laughing. It's a gangster move, frankly.'

'Ha, thanks,' I say.

'I think that's why Kareena went hard on you. She told me afterwards she wanted you to rinse me to my face. Apparently it's not good television to just play a YouTube video everyone's already seen. Also, you're a teenager so what do you know about the world? She wanted to replicate the whole scenario. I legit thought she wanted me to get an apology. And I thought you were in on it. I just, you know? I thought we were all on the same page about the joke.'

'Sounds like we were all part of different jokes. And that was partly on Kareena.'

It's nice talking to Marvin like this, just listening to him. He's sweeter and more thoughtful than I realised and, cheating aside, I can see why Shanai likes him. Maybe Papa was right and I need to listen before jumping to conclusions.

'Yeah, man. They didn't take care of us. They even told me I was getting your dressing room and they were going to make you wait in the corridor, to make you madder. And I thought, neither of us know anything about dressing rooms, I think she'll be fine.'

'Did Kareena say anything about me?'

'Nah, not really. She knew you were mad. She said to one of her producers that she thought you'd be funnier and it was a disappointment you weren't.'

'She said that?'

'Innit. Kept saying sorry to them. Looked really embarrassed.'

'Rah,' I say. It gives me an idea. I say goodbye to Marvin and run off into the building.

The hardest part of filming a video while pretending to be on the toilet is balancing the camera at the right angle to make it convincing you're on the toilet without giving the game away, but also not angling so it's just pointing up at you. I don't carry a tripod around with me for emergency toilet-gag filming opportunities.

I get the selfie angle right. You can see the cistern. You can see the depressing white tiles. You can hear the echo.

I have taken my influence from beefing rappers recording diss tracks to each other, sending for each other over record. They have a few hours to respond. And that's it. We're off to the rap races. Settle in with some popcorn and await the gleam of sweat on the rappers' faces as they try to bring the better bars.

'Oh,' I say, straight down the lens of the camera, smirking. 'You thought I was dead? You thought you got me? Yo, Kareena Patel, listen. Listen up. You thought some sort of humiliation of young brown girls was acceptable behaviour? Why? Cos you're scared of the competition? Want to be the only brown girl in the room? Well, I challenge you to a comedy death match. You hear me? Comedy Death Match. You, me, ten minutes, a set of your choosing. Do one of your hits if you want. That'd be cute. Like your wah-wah-my-Mum-hates-that-I'm-a-goofy-artist bit. Or something new. Either way, you and me, we're going toe-to-toe. If you win, well, you'll have proven yourself to be better than a seventeen year old. If I win, well, I get to lord it over you for a long time. You are my butler for a week. And you apologise to my family on television. Oh, and buy all my textbooks for first year of uni. Second-hand is fine. You have one week. Meet me at LOLZ, in Bristol. Next Friday. Eight p.m. Goodbye.'

I turn the camera up to the ceiling, press the flush and switch it off.

I upload it to Twitter, @ her into it and go about my day because those A levels won't study themselves. And with a sentence like that, I need all the help I can get.

The video goes viral quickly. Like, not in a pleasant way. Lots of people retweeting it, my only tweet, from my reactivated account. They all say the same sort of thing. The nerve of this little girl. They're all men who say it, the grossness of it all makes me feel ill.

229

Kareena quote tweets it with a laughing emoji. **Should I?** she asks.

The replies are a mixture of 'Yes, crush the evil child' and 'Nah, don't bother with the arrogant child'.

I try to not spend my day distracted by this gambit but I've realised something, which is: why I'm doing this. I don't need Kareena and I don't need to beat her or avenge myself. I need comedy and I need my family. I let both of them down. Yes, ladies and gentlemen, I let comedy down, man. I let it straight down.

Kareena accepts the challenge later that day and I text Leila, who is like, 'We are already on the case this is amazing wow wow wow woah woah woah comedy roast'.

I don't really need to defeat Kareena. I just need to do my best and take the opportunity I was initially given.

Papa was right, Meena was right, damn, even Marvin was right. I have been obsessing over what's missing from my voice. And maybe it's me. I'm missing.

Jazz texts me asking when I need him to train me. I tell him no. No training required. I know what needs to be done. Just show up and enjoy, man.

I invite Mum and Papa and Meena and Saeed. Something weird happened when Meena left. A few hours later, when I assumed she was on the train, she added us all to a family WhatsApp group. We're all in a family WhatsApp group, and Saeed is there, and it's mostly videos of Kavita and forwards from Mum. But it's such a comfort. My only contribution so far, other than versions of 'OMG cute' at my niece, is to invite them to my gig. They all agree to come.

I invite them, and Danny and Jazz and Shanai and Marvin. I fill the room up. I invite Adibah and Bella and the others from Hidden Corner. This is going to be the moment I emerge, voice intact. I run through all the things that have happened to me this past month: failing my first stand-up, finding my feet in front of a receptive audience, allowing myself to be humiliated on Kareena's show, humiliating my family, Papa's heart attack, my uni woes – all the way through to money being tight because my lack of attention to my waiting job this month has produced a significant reduction in tips.

I figure I've always hidden this part of me. This amazing, beautiful part of me that makes me me, the part that not only helps me move forward in the world, but also helps me speak the truth of myself to people. If I continue to hide it from those close to me, what chance do I have of making it out there, in the wider world?

If I can perform comedy to a room of people I know, respect and love, and Kareena Patel, that's the hardest room there is. And every other room after that will be easier than this. They'll still be hard. But surmountably so. Because I got through this.

Even if I bomb.

Even if I freeze.

Even if I say something that someone takes personally.

They will still know me.

28

I'll tell you a secret, ladies and gentlemen. Only between you and me. You won't tell anyone, will you? Especially not my enemies or specifically, my nemesis. Isn't that a weird old thing? You can have enemies, people you are against, people who stand for the opposite of what you stand for. You can have friends, aka the people who know to take their shoes off when they enter your house and would accept a call from you if you needed to move a dead body. You have frenemies you need to keep close. And you have a nemesis, who is basically the person who will be responsible for your downfall. But you never have a frenemesis. Right? Also, my nemesis is me. No one will ever be more responsible for my downfall than me.

Anyway, you won't tell any of those people if I tell you a secret, right?

Here's the secret: I really hate sandwiches. A sandwich for me is the exact epitome of Britishness. A delicious filling like cheese or ham or something, pressed together by soggy white things.

Gross.

Typical British behaviour: wrap everything up in soggy white things.

* * *

It's a long bus journey to LOLZ the following Friday. Not because I'm nervous. Traffic is just really terrible. As my stop approaches, I stand up and walk to the front of the top deck. I swivel on the pole and bounce down the stairs.

Tonight is the night and the fact that it's happening is more important than how it goes.

Bristol feels like a city on the brink of warfare tonight. There are three separate protests happening across the centre, the police horse patrol is out and boys weave in and out of the melee of people on electric scooters. Somewhere, someone is belting out a tuneless, shouty rendition of 'Red Red Wine' by UB40 and the chatter of people as they move from place to place is confident and assertive. I move through the crowd anonymously till I hit Nelson Street, walking down it, past the trainer shop and the record shop, and the taco place that spills out on to more than its fair share of the pavement, and I see LOLZ.

Back to where it all started.

When I arrive at the venue, I spot Jazz at the bar with Leila, both of them leaning over his phone. The way he looks at her while she looks at the screen makes me feel surprisingly jealous. I also then feel bad interrupting them to get Leila's attention, and, as promised, she leads me into the staff room, between the bar and the toilets – often mistakenly entered, once even defiled with urine.

Leila has turned it into a makeshift green room. There are

packets of Haribo decanted into cereal bowls, pint glasses of peanuts and some diet soft drinks in a can for me, clearly labelled 'MADHU (talent)' and a bottle of red wine labelled 'Kareena'. I sit down and readjust my ponytail so the hairs that have frazzled out of it after a stressful bus ride can return to their pals.

'What do you want me to do when Kareena arrives?' Leila says.

'Let her in, she's talent too.'

I sit by myself for twenty minutes, gathering my thoughts. I know what I want to say and to who and what about. I have a couple of killer punchlines. But the free flow. This is what I want to learn. I don't want to script myself. I want to work it out till the joke appears. Do the work in front of people. That's what matters. I've read enough thoughts about process to tell me that this is the way most of these cats do it.

I stand up and I walk around the room. I create a little Post-it note treasure hunt for Leila for when she's bored. The first one is a Post-it on the computer screen, laying out the challenge, and there are five more to find. At the end is a Post-it note with a heart on it saying she's wonderful and maybe she should just ask Jazz out because they obviously like each other and neither of them seem to possess the correct forward momentum to just say the words, 'date me'.

I straighten up some books by alphabetising them. They're a collection that've been left in the bar. I pick one up and skim through it. It's a collection of essays by a bunch of PoCs. I pick one out by Nish Kumar and scan through it. I've read these before but it feels like a comfort, a transaction of ideas through the prism of laughter from one comedian to the other.

I'm putting it back on the shelf when the door opens and I fumble the replacing of the volume, making it look like I'm guiltily reading something I shouldn't. Leila enters first and softly beckons Kareena into the room.

She walks in, straight-backed, lips pursed, hands on her hips, like, I cannot believe I'm being made to do this. She's wearing a black T-shirt and black jeans, white kicks; hers more immaculate than mine.

I look at her and nod. She nods back, before looking away.

Feeling the awkwardness, Leila backs out of the room like an articulated lorry.

'Oh, god,' I say and Kareena whips her head round to look at me. 'This is so embarrassing, we dressed the same. How will the audience tell the two brown girls apart?'

I laugh but Kareena gives me nothing. She sits down and grabs her phone from the bum bag holding court across her body and scrolls through it.

'I can't believe you came alone.'

'I can't believe I came,' she says, not looking up. I feel her eyes flick up to me and down. It's an act. 'My managers are outside setting up the camera crew.'

'What camera crew?'

235

'Oh, I record everything. Don't worry. I doubt we'll show your bit.'

I laugh and sit down opposite her.

She looks up at me over the top of her phone and gestures with a quick chin flick for me to tell her what's so funny.

'Oh, well, you're acting like the injured party. This was all totally optional. You could have just not come.'

Kareena drops her hands and leans forward.

'You called me out, online. I don't take that lightly. It's not exactly worth my time lording it up over a seventeen year old. But, I guess, a call out is a call out.'

She leans back again.

I sit and watch her for a bit. I don't think she's nervous, I don't think she's unhappy. For some reason, she feels like she owes me this and she's here against her will. Good.

I don't want her to enjoy this. I'm not. I'm doing it because it needs to be done. I open up a can of one of my soft drinks and sip from it, going through some notes in my notebook. I'm going to write my set down again so I can remember it just before we start.

Kareena reaches across the table to grab the other can and I look at her, before moving it closer to me.

'That's my rider.' I point to her bottle of wine. 'That's yours.'

'What's your power play here? Get me drunk?'

'No,' I say, sipping slowly. 'You can choose to do what you want. I'm not here to make you feel comfortable. It's like I'm purposefully not putting you in a dressing room to get you all weirded out.'

Kareena laughs.

'That boy, what's his name? Martin . . . ?'

'Marvin,' I correct her.

'Yeah, what – he's been spilling the secrets, has he? So what? What do you want me to do about it? Say sorry? I'm making television. I don't need to make it nice or likeable or anything. It just needs to be what people will watch.'

'I know,' I say. 'Listen, thanks for doing this. It means a lot.'

'It's my pleasure,' she says, staring at her phone.

'When you apologise to my family on television,' I reply. 'Remember to pronounce all their names properly.'

Kareena laughs, like, *Oh, OK, Madhu is serious*, and the thought that she is finally taking me seriously thrills me. It's such a conflicting feeling: she still means the world to me even after everything she has done. And I leave the room to conserve my power as the person who gave her no choice. Thanos would be so proud of me. This gig was inevitable.

The crowd is jumping, jumping, shout-outs to Destiny's Child. Mum and Papa and Saeed and Meena sit in the middle, Marvin and Shanai stand at the back. People from Hidden Corner all stand by the bar, letting Adibah hold court. So many people have come out.

Jazz approaches me. He's about to speak and then Leila shouts something across the room at him that makes no sense to me. It's an in-joke, probably.

'Christ, just go out with her already,' I say.

'Wait, what?' he says. 'She's not . . . well, I mean, she's not the . . . How you feeling, superstar?' He quickly changes the subject.

I feel a flutter in my chest, and something creeps towards me, a quiet realisation I need to park for later. Game face for now.

I nod, silently breathing in the same air as so many people I know. I note the cameramen filming the stage, the sound engineer trying to make sense of the small rig the venue has. I stare at the stage and grip Jazz's hands tighter as he tries to release himself.

'You're going to compère tonight,' I tell him. 'I asked Sam to let you and he was ecstatic. Tell some jokes, set the vibe right, bring her on and then me. Don't make it weird that she's opening for me. Just make it a fact. It's what's happening. Don't reference what went down on the television show. Just be funny, be yourself, bring us up, and we'll all have a nice time and then I'll take you out for some pizza at Pizza City afterwards because there's no way I can afford to buy you anything else. OK?'

'I've never compèred before,' Jazz says, his voice getting higher and higher. 'Adibah is right there. Ask her.'

'You're good,' I tell him, smile and return to the green room to give Kareena the warning that it's all about to go down.

29

'Good evening, ladies and gentlemen . . . I am your host Jazz Jhooti. Nice to see you. Welcome to LOLZ at The Station. I am going to lead you through this amazing gig. In years to come, people will be like, I was there, I witnessed the birth of a legend. But there's, like, one hundred or so of you in here. You'll know the truth. Take a look to your right, and to your left. In front, and behind. Remember these faces. You were the ones who witnessed the night our headliner Madhu Krishna became a star.'

Whoops from the middle of the crowd – my mum and my sister – reach my ears as I lean against the bar. Kareena is huddled with her managers.

I watch Jazz open proceedings with ease. He is more relaxed than I thought. He's making himself laugh, doing crowd work. He's asking people their jobs and then reminding them he's a student, leading him to a riff on how his dream job is to be a mattress influencer. He makes a couple of accidental innuendos, which he tries to riff on but fails, and so he leans back into the main joke: that he is lazy and he needs a daytime job to supplement the comedy. We all laugh.

Kareena walks over to me with one of her managers, who stands next to her as she watches the stage.

'Listen,' Kareena says to me. 'I know you think you know what's going to happen next. But I just want you to know, I'm going to obliterate you in front of your family, your friends and my camera operators. I bet you'll wish I stayed at home.'

I'm counting on this.

'It's the extra effort it takes to be horrible that I don't understand,' I reply, as Jazz starts laying out Kareena's bio, to whoops and hollers.

'Then you've never been the only one who looks like you in your industry before.'

'And I never will be,' I say. 'Cos if I make it, I'm making space for everyone I can.'

'Lol,' she says, the ultimate insult. 'Good luck with that, sis.'

'Good luck up there, sis,' I say.

If I were to watch myself out of my body, tussling with Kareena Patel, I would not believe it. My sister's words are in my ears though. Why do I care what this person thinks or says? Instead, I am taking the opportunity I should have taken before.

I suddenly feel like my chest has been filled with hot air, you know, like in heated swimming pools, where the hot condensation has replaced normal air and gone, take a hike kid.

I try to breathe and I try to breathe and I try to breathe and then Kareena Patel is introduced. She bounces on stage with the energy and vigour of a seasoned pro who wants to rescue the night from a bad compère, and she picks up the mic and holds her arms out for rapturous supportive applause throughout the full room.

'Bristol,' she says. 'My home town, it's been too long! It's been so long that last time I was here, gigging, you guys had all the slave owner statues everywhere. Now? In the harbour, mate. Last time I was here, all the Banksys looked like they'd been thrown up the night before. Last time I was here, Massive Attack was still the Wild Bunch.'

People roar with laughter at her easy local-knowledge jokes.

'And now I'm back, headlining for my nemesis, Madhu Krishna. If you want to know the type of person I am, know that. If my nemesis calls me out on social media and demands I support their first ever headline slot, I'm there. My therapist calls this my desperation to please. My mum calls it . . . why-haven't-you-called-me-in-two-days syndrome. I refer to it as masochism. Imagine, imagine having a nemesis, first of all. Sure. Now, imagine they're seventeen. Because I do not want a seventeen-year-old nemesis. Know how dangerous that is? Cos if she goes on TikTok, I'm screwed. If she goes on TikTok and says, Kareena Patel is cancelled, man, they would come for me quicker than our prime minister to a golf tournament. Listen, I'm not kidding. Luckily, the nemesis who picked me is Madhu, right? Only my nemesis could get me to open for her. Me? I've been in this business for years, over a decade. And yet, here I am, opening for my nemesis. How the mighty have fallen? No. How the mighty have the worst nemeses. I mean, listen, I could be literally doing anything else right now. I could be eating takeaway at home in my pants and a comfier black T-shirt than this one, playing my PlayStation, murking people on the internet. But why am I here? Consider this my last stand against my nemesis. Boys and girls, binaries and non-binaries, this ends here. This battle we've locked in for, well, let's face it, two weeks now, is over. Two weeks in teen years, is what? A decade? And isn't it past her bedtime? Does her Mum know she's out? Actually, you know what? I think her Mum's in the audience right now. So, don't worry everyone. My nemesis brought her chaperone. She has parental consent for this school trip. Because . . . well . . .' Kareena says, smiling, pausing before she launches into another series of one-liners about my age, and how young I am, and I'm standing at the back going, is that all you got? I'll get older, but you'll always be mean. How on earth did I respect this person? Kareena finishes her run, to scattered laughter, and pauses, smiling at us all. 'Look, I'm glad you're laughing, cos that's all you're going to get today. Cos when my nemesis comes on, wowee, you'll be able to hear mice debate Brexit it'll be so quiet. Know what I mean? Great, OK, listen, I am the only comedian you need to care about. Watch my show, Madhu. You'll never make it – face it, love. Goodnight!'

Kareena drops the mic and walks off stage and I realise I haven't moved for the ten minutes she's been up there. All the noise in my head has filtered into the same frequency where her voice and the laughter riding it are all at the same volume. She looks at me like she has slain me. I stand here, propped up by the sword she has driven through me, a blade so thorough, it pierces the ground behind me. I have to remember how the crowd reacted. And that whatever my feelings towards Kareena are, were, that this shouldn't affect my performance.

She winks at me. And I feel like she has won. What am I doing? This was always about showing her I was good, wasn't it? And now I have to go up there and rebut her every accusation about me, about my generation, worst of all about what people are allowed to find funny. It's an absolute catastrophe. How could I have done this to my hero? This is nerves talking. Surely. *Remember what she did to you*, I whisper to myself inside my brain.

Right.

Enough.

I remind my brain that I am a comedy god. I. Am. A. Comedy. God.

Jazz smiles at the audience and I try to calm my breathing, remembering the technique Danny taught me.

In for a count of four, out for a count of eight. In for a count of four, out for a count of eight.

'Wow,' Jazz says. 'Someone came here for a fight. I thought it was a comedy evening. That's the thing about these sorts of events – everyone thinks everyone else is in competition with them. But it's up to you to decide, you the audience. So listen, tonight is a very special night. I have known this comic for, well, a couple of months, and no one has made me laugh harder than her except, well, you know that meme of Homer

Simpson backing into a bush. Gets me every time. Here she is, almost funnier than the Homer Simpson backing into a bush gif, you've seen her on television, now see her rock your comedy world . . . it's Madhu Krishna!'

The crowd erupts into rapturous, welcoming, warm applause. Adibah is whooping and hollering, Papa is on his feet, beaming. Kareena smirks and says, 'Good luck up there,' as she heads into the green room.

I am jolted forward by some hands behind me and that pulls me back into the room, my body awake, my limbs suddenly operating with intent and motion, and I look behind me at Leila, smiling. I see Kareena hovering in the door. She wants to know what happens next. And I look at her and I think, *You know what, this room, which is my world, needs to know what she's like and how she has been the worst nightmare ever.*

Never ever meet your heroes.

Never.

I run on to stage and grab the microphone from Jazz and stare out into the darkness where the crowd is. And I say hello and then I freeze.

Because every ounce of me wants to cuss her. And destroy her and bring her down and make everyone laugh about what an embittered sell-out she is.

'Listen, hi,' I say. 'Yes, I am Kareena's nemesis, and you know what?'

I pause.

In the silence, I can hear people get their phones out, people lean forward to hear my truth, people clear their throats nervously. What is she going to say about Kareena Patel?

This is the moment I say something I'm going to regret for the rest of my life, guys.

'Kareena Patel can go suck her mum, you know . . .'

I say it thinking I'm going to get a laugh and all I get is a gasp. A collection of gasps. And in the gasps, I find myself in a cave.

It's a metaphorical cave, ladies and gentlemen, go with me. I'm wading through the darkness. I can hear a bear behind me and I can see the embers of daylight up ahead but the more I wade towards the light, the further away it seems, like it's a trick of my imagination and the bear is actually blocking the way out. The air is thick and dusty and coating my lungs with some sort of cave dust. And the bear's growls sound like a whole party of them, out on the hunt, looking for someone to maul. And so I quicken my step and I'm trapped. The light I was running towards has disappeared. And the bear's breath is on my neck.

I freeze. I drop the microphone. I just drop it on the floor. It clunks and does that feedback wail you only really hear in the movies.

In the ensuing silence, I realise I have no option but to run, to get off the stage, to just go. But my body is frozen to the spot. I cannot move . . . anything. Not my brain, my hands, my feet. I am just stuck.

I have failed.

Wait.

Stop.

I just told Kareena Patel to go suck her mum and then I froze. This is not what this is about. Come on, Madhu.

The spotlight is blinding, and I'm still in the cave, but the bear has eaten me now, and I don't know if imaginary cave bears even have a taste for human flesh, but there you go, and the whiteness of the spotlight is me accepting my fate and ascending to heaven – because despite it all, I'm a good person.

No.

Wait.

Stop.

Ladies and gentlemen.

Stop.

I ain't going out like that. I crouch down and pick up the microphone. I bounce back up and smile audibly into it.

'That was awkward,' I say. 'Starting with that. You know, like this is a battle roast or something where I'm going toe-to-toe with a professional comedian when I actually just wanted to tell you a story about my family.' People laugh, relief washes over them. 'My dad has this annoying habit of leaving all the lights on in the house. I walk behind him as he leaves every room, being like, Papa, it's not Diwali, Papa, it's not a party . . . Papa, you'll be dead soon and then the ice caps will flood all the light fittings if you keep doing this. It was a funnier joke when my dad wasn't nearly dying. Wait, he's not dying.

He's in the audience right now. Not dying. Very much alive. But we had a health scare. It turns out,' I say, meeting Papa's eyes and, seeing the sparkle in them, I carry on through. 'It turns out . . . his tension at his daughter shouting at him to turn the lights off all the time gave him a heart attack. Just a little one. Just a mild one. Just a forty-eight-hours-of-sympathy one. He didn't have an oh-god-time-to-research-hospices heart attack, nor did he have a well-I-guess-we'll-switch-his-diet-to-celery-and-watch-as-he-buys-a-convertible-and-asks-his-secretary-out-on-a-date heart attack. Just a mini one. Just enough of one to remind me how annoying it'd be if he died. Cos if he died, I'd have to deal with that electricity bill. Which is going to be huge because I'm never turning a light off as long as I live.'

People are laughing. Rolling with laughter. It's all in the delivery, the pauses, the exaggeration, the way I act out Papa's heart attacks, the way I play insolent teenage daughter. And people are rolling about.

'My family's weird though, right? Anyone else got a weird family?' People whoop. I can hear the shuffling about of people putting their hands up. 'Have you ever considered, those of you brave enough to admit your family's weird . . . that you're the weird one? Because I'm starting to think I'm the weird one. Firstly, I'm solving family crises through stand-up comedy. This was all a ruse to get them all into one room again and say, please please can we stop fighting every Christmas? We love each other, we do, we do. Secondly, I'm the least funny person in my family. Seriously, my mum, she don't say much, but when she does, she will cut you down to size. She met my friend Jazz recently, and she said afterwards, "He always notices a mirror in any room". Like, what a genius thing to say about him. Of course he does, you saw him up here – he's a pretty boy who, if he dyed his hair blonde, you'd realise his hair twin is Bart Simpson. Mum also once told me that the reason I'm so loud is because I spent my childhood competing with loud Bollywood music from my dad's stereo. So if I wanted him to know I was hungry, or I'd pooped myself, or that I was still alive, I had to be really loud. Louder than Lata. And Lata's loud, man, she's so shrill, dogs are fluent in Hindi. Ever say to a dog, bes bes? It'll go down much faster than if you bark "sit" at it.' I don't know where this riffing is coming from at this point. I'm just lost in the moment. 'Here's a truth about me. I speak loudly because I don't always know what to say and sometimes, making noise is better than silence, right? And how many of us – I'm talking to the ethnics now, to the women of colour out there, to my marginalised folks – how many of us take the first excuse to sit down and shut up, right? It's what we've been conditioned to do. Not be noticed. I don't know what the future holds, friends. But I do know this, I'll only speak when I know what to say. Lucky for you, lads, I always know what to say. So my final message to everyone is, go and get yourself humiliated on national television. It doesn't really inspire creativity but it reminds you who around you is important and will help you stand up and say things.

And if anyone in the audience wants to chat comedy with me, just see me afterwards. This movement is not just one person, one unicorn eating all the grass. It's a big field, there's enough grass for all of us. This isn't a reference to illegal substances. Goodnight!'

I hand the microphone to Jazz, who bounds on to the stage to hype the crowd to cheer me off. And you know what? The reaction is so wild. People are cheering and throwing up gun fingers and clapping and all sorts of things. I know it wasn't laugh-a-minute. But it's a start.

Kareena stands there, leaning against the wall, arms crossed, nodding slowly at me. I walk past her and then stop in front of her.

'You may see me as your nemesis but I don't see you as mine. I see you as someone who made this seem possible for me. And that's it.'

'You owe me a thank you, it seems,' Kareena says, smirking. 'For helping you with your confidence issues. You're gonna be great. Remember to thank me in your memoir.'

'I did all this myself,' I tell her. 'Because I know what I'm about. Do you?'

I walk away, knowing I won't see a reaction on her face but it'll be there, the truth gnawing at her. She was my hero. In many ways, she still is.

I call out after her, without looking back. 'Don't forget to apologise to my family. Oh, and the textbooks! Second-hand is fine!' People around me laugh.

I look for Meena, Mum and Papa in the crowd and run to them.

I hug my sister as Papa bangs my shoulder and tells me I'm funny. I feel happy and I feel satisfied and also I feel like I know what I need to do to get better – and that's all I ever really needed. The confidence to get up again and again and not be afraid of it going badly, and always, always, always, sticking to my voice.

Over Meena's shoulder, I see Jazz, smiling at me, beaming, almost. It's not like his usual proud-uncle smile. This time it feels different.

Not thinking it through too much, just going with the feeling, I release Meena and walk over to Jazz and grab his face, pulling it down towards mine till our lips meet.

30

Let's just assume some time passes between then and the next bit I want to tell you about before we finish up.

In that period, Jazz and I go on a bunch of dates and hit up a bunch of open mics and we get closer and closer and we spend a lot of time either kissing or laughing at each other. It feels easy. Like he's someone I've known my whole life and I've been waiting to know my whole life. More than a friend, or a boyfriend, just a kindred spirit. He is kind and supportive and never competitive, and makes me laugh.

Meena and Saeed move back to Bristol. Turns out, London is expensive and Saeed can't study and work, and Meena is finding it hard to find work that fits around baby stuff, so Mum and Papa decide to help them out and do childcare. That means hiring someone. So money is a bit tighter now, but they're happier. The new person they hire revolutionises the stock, goes all local and starts stocking produce like Bristol honey, Somerset cheese, Weston milk and so on, and suddenly it's a shop awash with people. It's busy and actually profits are better than one might expect.

Jazz gets an offer from King's College in London, to study

English. And I work hard at my studies. I have my sights set on London. I want to check out the London comedy scene. Like what Papa said about how he and I both make our minds up about the world without checking it first. Maybe I need to check the world out first. And then make jokes about it. That's why I'm looking at a politics course in London too. Jazz and I do two gigs a week that summer. We do the Hidden Corner open mic every week and we both promise to always try out new stuff – sometimes with success, mostly with absolute and complete failure, but a nugget and a kernel forming. We also pick the open mics in the South West and hit them up. We both go to do one in London but the spots are all full by the time we arrive, not realising that you pre-book online, and also, you have to know the compère. But we meet a few other comics our age that we hang with who've come up from Brighton for the same thing. We start a little 'young PoCs getting into comedy' WhatsApp group that slowly grows. I name it the Kareena Patel Appreciation Society when I set it up.

Kareena Patel carries on with her life. She probably doesn't give me another single thought. That's OK – the way I'm gigging, I'm sure our paths will cross again.

I still listen to her old stuff, but not as much as I used to. And actually, travelling around, doing more gigs is giving me the names of up-and-coming comics to try and I'm listening to and watching lots of new people now.

My vocabulary for comedy is growing. As is the likelihood of two As and a B. That'll get me to where I need to be. And I can continue my education and do gigs and just be consumed by both at the same time. That's entirely possible. It's all possible. All I need to do is just stand up, get on stage and talk. Slowly, slowly, I'm building towards my first five-minute set.

Speaking of which, I'll tell you a secret, ladies and gentlemen.

Your dog is cute, but only from a distance. I don't like how it smells my feet and paws me. People on the internet pay good money to do that sort of behaviour. I don't know what it is about dogs that made me so blah about them. Other than that I am a monster who deserves no sympathy. I guess the thing is, when it comes down to it . . . a dog is not a personality. Like dyeing your hair teal, or reading books, having a dog is not a personality. You know what *is* a personality? Being a cat lover.

I've been Madhu Krishna, you've been my audience. Goodnight, and good luck with whatever obstacles face you in the next twenty-four hours. After that, you're on your own.

Goodnight. Oh, and Kareena, if you're out there, remember: second-hand is fine.

Acknowledgements

Thank you to my agent Julia Kingsford and to Charlotte Atyeo for making this book a reality. Thank you to everyone at Hodder Children's Books for continuing to support my YA books: to Naomi Greenwood for the amazing thoughtful hilarious editorial steer (and for agreeing with me about pineapple on pizza being bad vibes), Sarah Lambert for acquiring the book, to Laura Pritchard for additional editorial support, to Emma Roberts for forensic copyediting (dream team back together!), to Emily Thomas for all the amazing publicity and Bec Gillies for the marketing. To Binita Naik for support on the audio side and to the amazing design team led by Michelle Brackenborough, and to Josephine Rais for the iconic cover illustration. Thank you to Adele Brimacombe for proofreading and to production controller, Joelyn Esdelle.

Thank you to Saima Ferdows for an early read and early thoughts on the book and on Madhu and on comedy. Thank you to all the stand-up comedians and comedy writers whose input, either direct or indirect, has influenced this story: Josie Long, Nish Kumar, Bisha K Ali, Kai Samra, Kemah Bob, Azam Mahmood.

Thank you to Bash Naran and Nish Panchal for being amazing. Thank you to Jessie Nelson for introducing me to my actual comedy hero, Larry David, once. Thanks to Himesh Patel and Nikesh Patel for thoughts on story. Thanks to the Council Of Good Friends: Nish Kumar, Musa Okwonga, Vinay Patel, Inua Ellams for being the best of the best. I find all of us very attractive. Thank you to Chimene Suleyman for your astonishing rock solid support every single day. Thank you to Rosie Knight and Nick Marino, and to Professor Madhu Krishnan, and to Nikita Gill, Anoushka Shankar and Nerm [last name redacted].

Thanks to everyone in my family, to K, S and C, the funniest people I know. And to all my sisters, who are the real Madhus, the ones who make me laugh and laugh and laugh and laugh, even if it's mostly at my expense. I love you all so dearly: Nishma, Shalini, Krupa, Leena, Priya, Reshma, Kavita, Meera. Thanks to Pallavi Sharda and Shruti Ganguly and Uzma Hasan, Tanya Byrne, Candice Carty-Williams and Tanaïs.

Finally, thanks to all the librarians, either in the community or in schools: the work you do is so incredibly vital. To teachers, thank you for supporting my work. And to all the young people, either in youth clubs, youth groups, schools or mentoring programmes I've gotten a chance to spend time with, thank you for all that you do.

Read on for an extract from

Run, Riot

11.42 p.m.

Sim stares at his laptop screen. He can't quite believe what he's watching. It's definitely Mr Johnson. And him. That man. With the angry voice. Unmistakeable. Sim can't focus on the words he's shouting at Mr Johnson, he's too surprised to see the man there. The blows to Mr Johnson's face, his chest, sound painful. Sim winces. He wants to look away but he can't.

He feels tears froth in his eyes.

He rubs at his newly shorn head and feels the bristles against his fingertips. He lets the tears come. How could that man do this to his mentor? That man from NextGen Properties was beating on Mr Johnson. Then, into frame comes another face Sim recognises. A copper. Inspector Blakemore.

Sim looks around the top deck of the bus that's taking him back to his neighbourhood. No one is there. Not at this time of night. Sim's head is all over the place.

This NextGen guy's supposed to be a businessman, Sim thinks. *This violence. It's just . . . it's too much.*

But it proves Mr Johnson is innocent.

Sim feels an angry burn in his chest as the bus nears his stop. He ejects the USB stick containing the video files and buries it in the pocket of his long puffa coat. He stands up, steadying himself on the back of the seat in front of him. His knees feel weak.

NextGen, Sim thinks.

He steps off the bus and looks over at Firestone House, his home since the day he was born. He hears the low murmur of people across the road. He nods when he sees it's CJ and one of his guys. Sim walks towards Firestone House, unsteady, trying to process what he's just seen. The video. He was surprised enough to hear from the sender, but never in a million years did he expect this. What does it mean? And how did the sender come across it in the first place?

And what in god's name should he do next? He has to confront Patterson, surely. Give the man an opportunity to come clean before he's exposed. Get Mr Johnson free.

Sim approaches the entrance to his tower block, looks up the fourteen floors to the top and blows a kiss, like he always does when he comes home.

'You're late,' he hears.

He spots Taran, in the shadows, leaning against a wall. She smiles and readjusts the cap on her head. She walks up to him, arms outstretched for a hug.

Sim accepts the hug, linking his fingers around Taran's back. As she rests her cheek on his chest, he stares at the ground over her shoulder, unsure what to do now, knowing that what he has just seen on the screen of his laptop is going to change everything.

5.40 p.m.

However it starts, it has to be loud.

Taran whispers this to herself as she pushes the door leading to the roof wide open. The door swings back on its hinges as she stomps through and then bangs shut behind her. Like a kick drum.

Whatever happens, it has to happen big. Big start, maximum repetition for effect, slow build, big chorus... No – scratch that – an unbelievably big anthem-like chorus and, at the centre of it, her bars.

Because she's not messing about. This is her year. Her time to shine. She's done the odd verse on the odd mixtape here and there. And there's been the odd bit of heat. And people keep telling her they're waiting. Now it's time to release things. It's all she can think about, recording. Every day, that's all she wants to do. Record bars.

Producer? Check my microphone levels, run the beat, let me loose.

Give me the stage. In fact, why am I even going to that gig tonight when I could own any of the rappers on that stage?

Except Rage. No one is as good as Rage.

Taran is going by 'Riot' now. She's settled. That's her MC name. Riot. It's because every bar is the soundtrack to a riot, every syllable is dissent and every rhyme is an exploding grenade. *Riot.* The more she says it to herself, the more she loves it. She hasn't told the guys yet.

She's keeping it close in her heart. Like that Warren Zevon song her dad used to play over and over again – 'Keep Me in Your Heart'. Damn, just thinking about that song hurts. She asked Cody to sample it but when he played her the beat she just ran out of the studio cos she couldn't breathe.

Anyway, 'Run'. That tune, the one she was working on today, it's called 'Run'. 'Run' by Riot. Sick.

Her cap is pulled down low over her eyes so she doesn't see Anna stood in front of her, staring out into the middle distance. The first sign she has of her best friend's presence is when Anna says, 'Can you see that?'

Taran looks up and sees Anna is pointing. She follows the arm to the finger to the nail to the skyline across the city.

'We can see the weather approaching from here,' Taran's twin brother Hari often says. 'We know what's coming and what's gone. We're the present.'

Hari doesn't say much. He likes to be the strong silent type. But every now and then he'll go all poetic and say abstract shit like that. Like he's competing with his rapper sister. He wrote a sonnet for Jamal to give to Anna one time for Valentine's Day, and now he thinks he's a big man of letters, like a Shakespeare or even an Akala or something. Really, Taran's the poet. Hari's the fighter. The funny thing is, Jamal never even gave Anna the poem cos it was so bad.

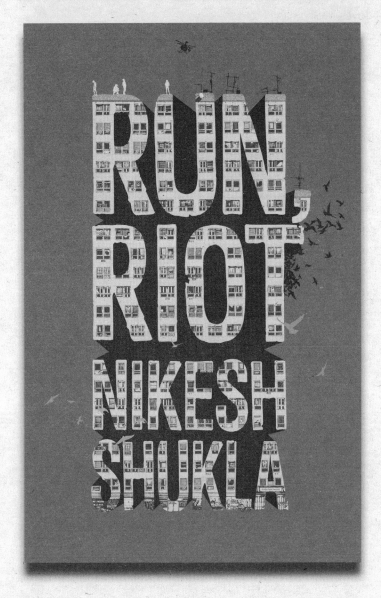

RUN, RIOT

NIKESH SHUKLA

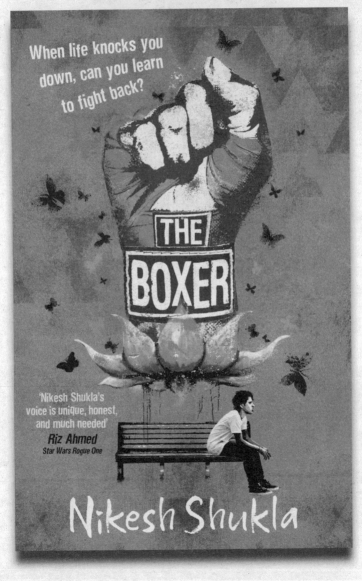

NIKESH SHUKLA

is the editor of British Book Award-shortlisted anthology *The Good Immigrant*, a collection of essays by British writers of colour about race and immigration in the UK. His debut novel, *Coconut Unlimited*, was shortlisted for the Costa First Novel Award and his debut YA novel, *Run, Riot*, was shortlisted for the Specsavers National Book Award. Nikesh has written for the *Guardian*, *Observer*, *Independent*, *Esquire*, *Buzzfeed*, *Vice*, BBC2 and BBC Radio 4. Nikesh was one of *Foreign Policy* magazine's 100 Global Thinkers and *The Bookseller*'s 100 most influential people in publishing in 2016 and in 2017. He is the co-founder of the literary journal, *The Good Journal* and The Good Literary Agency.